**Ten years had passed
since the three cousins
had all been in one place.**

Anne studied her cousin Bret's profile.
In silhouette her small nose tilted, chin lifted
defiantly, the incredible long, curved lashes
fanned upward over wide, gray-blue eyes.
In those long-ago summers the three girls had
spent together with their grandmother at her
beach cottage, Spindrift, Bret had been the
prettiest, most popular girl.

Still attractive, her cinnamon-brown hair
styled in a fashionable blunt cut, with her
smart pantsuit, Bret could have stepped
straight out of the pages of a fashion magazine
as the dressed-for-success career woman.

Anne found herself wondering what the last
ten years had been like for Bret. For their other
cousin, Lesley, as well. Maybe she'd have a
chance to find out before they all went their
separate ways again....

Books by Jane Peart

Love Inspired

The Risk of Loving #1
Promises To Keep #43
Sandcastles #242

Steeple Hill Single Title

Circle of Love

JANE PEART

Award-winning novelist Jane Peart is the author of over fifty books of inspirational and historical fiction and romance.

SANDCASTLES

JANE PEART

Published by Steeple Hill Books™

STEEPLE HILL BOOKS

Steeple
Hill®

ISBN 0-373-87252-6

SANDCASTLES

Copyright © 2004 by Jane Peart

All rights reserved. Except for use in any review, the reproduction
or utilization of this work in whole or in part in any form by any
electronic, mechanical or other means, now known or hereafter
invented, including xerography, photocopying and recording, or in
any information storage or retrieval system, is forbidden without
the written permission of the editorial office, Steeple Hill Books,
233 Broadway, New York, NY 10279 U.S.A.

All characters in this book have no existence outside the imagination of
the author and have no relation whatsoever to anyone bearing the same
name or names. They are not even distantly inspired by any individual
known or unknown to the author, and all incidents are pure invention.

This edition published by arrangement with Steeple Hill Books.

® and TM are trademarks of Steeple Hill Books, used under license.
Trademarks indicated with ® are registered in the United States Patent
and Trademark Office, the Canadian Trade Marks Office and in other
countries.

Visit us at www.steeplehill.com

Printed in U.S.A.

Ask, and it will be given to you; seek, and you will
find; knock, and the door will be opened to you.
For everyone who asks receives; he who
seeks finds; and to him who knocks,
the door will be opened.
—*Matthew* 7: 7-8

PROLOGUE

September

Two days after Lenora Sherwood's death, Bernessa Williams let herself into the Greenbrae, North Carolina, house where she had been housekeeper for the past thirty years. The family would begin arriving for the funeral soon, and Bernessa wanted to have everything in readiness. She knew how Miss Nora liked things done and she was determined to do them even though her mistress had passed. Fresh linens on all the beds in the four upstairs bedrooms, towels in the two bathrooms, downstairs the silver polished, china and crystal washed and ready for refreshments for the friends who would come to offer their condolences after the graveside ceremony.

Bernessa sighed as she got out her cleaning supplies from the cabinet in the big, sunny kitchen. She and Miss Nora had spent many an hour in this room, preparing food for family gatherings, canning the luscious peaches from the hillside orchards, baking dozens of holiday cookies and cakes to be taken to local nursing homes and shut-ins who were in Miss Nora's special care.

Looking around, Bernessa remembered as well the many other times they had just sat at the scrubbed pine table, drinking tea or coffee, talking. Been through a mighty lot together, she and Miss Nora.

Yes, Lord, good times and bad. They had shared their troubles, joys, sorrows and bewilderment at the ways of life. She glanced at the framed tri-cornered American flag in its place of honor over the desk. Bernessa remembered the day Miss Nora had received the news that her youngest son, a navy pilot, had been killed. It was the only time Bernessa had ever seen Miss Nora give way.

Now there were only two of her sons left to mourn her. The oldest, Randall, a lawyer, was in charge of all the funeral arrangements. He and his wife, Adele, were coming from nearby Larchmont. Their daughter, Lesley, would drive over from Wadesboro where she taught kindergarten.

Bernessa's gaze moved over to the photograph on the mantel taken when the three Sherwood sons were in their teens, handsome, blond, smiling. Miss Nora had set great store by those boys. Bernessa had watched them all grow up. Looked as alike as peas in a pod, yet each was as different from the other as day from night. Children! You just never knew. No matter how you tried to raise them, they all had their own paths to tread, as she knew well from her own.

"All we can do is pray, Bernessa," Miss Nora would say over and over at some news or other concerning one of her sons. She had grieved about Chandler's young widow and child after the plane crash that had taken his life. She'd taken Curtis's divorce hard. Miss Nora considered marriage a from-this-day-forward promise. She had worried particularly about Bretnay, only five at the time of her parents' breakup. "What's to become of a child growing up without a father—a father who chose to leave?" she would ask Bernessa. Not that she didn't worry about Anne, too, also growing up in a fatherless home. Lesley, her third granddaughter, seemed better off with two parents, even though she'd been fussed over too much by the mother, who had waited nearly eight years for a child.

When Bernessa told Miss Nora that she couldn't carry the weight of the world on her shoulders, she'd laugh and say, "You're right, Bernessa. Let go and let God. Keep reminding me of that, will you?"

In spite of Bernessa's repeated warnings about her taking on too much, Miss Nora went ahead and did as she pleased. Like the first year she invited all three grandchildren to spend the summer at her beach cottage, Spindrift.

At that announcement Bernessa had exclaimed "Now, Miss Nora, you don't want to do that! Summer's your time to relax. Three ten-year-olds! Why, they'll be full of beans, hoppin' and jumpin' and wantin' to be taken places, and there goes any chance you'll get of having yourself some rest. No Garden Club ladies luncheons to fix, no Missionary Society meeting, no choir practice—all your winter doin's."

But Miss Nora paid her no mind. The little girls came. Anne, all the way from California, a quiet child, with her father's long-lashed eyes and shy smile. Bret, smart, sassy and never still a minute. Bernessa couldn't rightly recall exactly where that child was living or which parent had custody just then. Lesley looked like one of those chubby tykes on the soup cans, rosy cheeked, curly-haired. Her mama had brought her, along with a jar full of multivitamins and a suitcase packed with pastel T-shirts and matching shorts.

Down on her knees now shining the brass andirons and fire screen, Bernessa chuckled. Don't think Lesley wore more'n two of those sets the whole summer.

Bernessa sat back on her heels. After that first year it became a regular thing. Every June the children arrived and stayed until Labor Day.

Those summer visits ended the year after the three graduated from high school. Of course, Lesley often came to visit Miss Nora here in Greenbrae with her parents. Her father, Randall, managed his mother's business and legal affairs. But none of the three granddaughters ever spent another summer at Spindrift. Not for ten years.

Whenever Bernessa asked about the girls or wondered out loud why they didn't visit or even write more letters to their grandmother, Miss Nora would hush her.

"Nonsense, Bernessa, they're busy young women with their own lives. College and careers and all sorts of interesting things to do, places to go. Why would they want to spend summers at a little cottage in an isolated beach town?"

Bernessa had shaken her head but not said more. She had her own opinion about the fact that the three didn't come. But she knew better than to say any more about it.

With some effort Bernessa got to her feet. A little stiff, these days. Well, what could you expect at sixty-seven? She went into the hall, got the vacuum out of the closet and plugged it in. Ten years. Hadn't seemed that long and yet time crept up on a person.

What were Anne and Bret like now that they were all grown up? What was it Miss Nora told her Anne did—worked at a college? And that scallawag Bret—what on earth had she been up to all these years? Plenty, Bernessa guessed, recalling some of her carryings-on that last summer at Spindrift. Of all the girls, it was Bret who troubled her grandmother most. Lesley, on the other hand, had lost her baby fat and become a lovely looking young lady. But way too thin. No bigger than a broomstick. Didn't eat enough to keep a bird alive. Even turned down Bernessa's biscuits and the banana pudding that used to be her favorite dessert the last time she was over to dinner with her grandmother. That was when she brought that fine young man she was engaged to. Funny thing, though, Miss Nora hadn't been too sure of that match. "I hope Lesley's doing what will make herself happy, Bernessa, not just pleasing her mother."

Too bad the other two hadn't somehow managed the time to come and visit their grandmother before now. There was time for tears and regret now, Bernessa reckoned. That went for Miss Nora's middle son, Curtis, Bret's father. Bernessa figured he'd been too upset after the first divorce to come, then, later, too embarrassed when there was a second one and a remarriage.

In spite of the fact that Randall and his family often came to Greenbrae, they rarely visited her at Spindrift. The cottage belonged to Miss Nora in more ways than this house. She had come to the house as a bride as many Sherwood brides before her had. But

Spindrift had been built for her by her husband, Dan, soon after they had their first baby. She loved that cottage and afterward spent every year from June to September there.

This year she had stayed longer than usual, telling Bernessa she hated to leave, saying this end of summer seemed more beautiful than any other she had ever known at the beach.

Finally, she had reluctantly packed up the station wagon and she and Bernessa had driven back to Greenbrae. She told Bernessa she planned to return to spend another week or so at Spindrift alone before closing the cottage for the winter.

Back at the Greenbrae house she and Bernessa were busy all morning settling in again. At noon she sent Bernessa home telling her she felt a little tired, that she was going to lie down for a short nap. A nap from which she never awoke.

It was a peaceful way to go. Bernessa recalled a remark Miss Nora once made upon the sudden death of a friend: "As long as you're in the state of grace, Bernessa. If you've walked with Him all along, you just take Jesus's hand and walk with Him into a brand-new life."

Yes, Lord, that was Miss Nora. Bernessa wiped away a few tears that rolled down her cheeks, feeling the loss of a dear, good friend.

An hour later Bernessa went out and locked the door behind her. She would come back early in the morning to have breakfast ready for the family members arriving for the funeral.

Part I

Chapter One

Anne Sherwood was relieved when the limousine provided by the mortuary drove through the stone pillars of Oak Hill Cemetery. She had shared the ride with her cousin Bret and Uncle Curtis, Bret's father. Although it had been only a short distance from the church to the cemetery, the trip had been extremely uncomfortable. The tension between Bret and her father, who'd been estranged for years, was tangible. After regarding her father with icy coldness, Bret had turned away to stare out the window.

Any attempt at conversation Anne made was met by a few banal replies from Uncle Curtis and stony silence from Bret. Finally Anne gave up.

Anne studied Bret's profile. In silhouette her small nose tilted, chin lifted defiantly, the incredible long curved lashes fanned upward over wide gray-blue eyes. In those long-ago summers they'd spent together with their grandmother at Spindrift, Bret had been the prettiest, most popular girl.

Still attractive, her cinnamon-brown hair styled in

a fashionable blunt cut, her pant suit smart, Bret could have stepped straight out of the pages of a fashion magazine as the dressed-for-success career woman.

Anne found herself wondering what the last ten years had been like for Bret. For their other cousin, Lesley, as well. Maybe she'd have a chance to find out before they all went their separate ways again.

Funerals were often stressful times where old wounds were reopened, where past conflicts resurfaced. The Sherwoods were probably no exception, especially since the family was so widely separated geographically, and by circumstances and lifestyles. Even finding a safe topic of conversation was difficult. Ten years, after all, was a long time. A lot could happen in a decade.

Anne herself felt numb. Nothing had seemed real since that early-morning call from Uncle Randall with the heartbreaking news of Nonie's death. The next few hours were frantic. Getting plane reservations from the small Northern California airport through San Francisco to North Carolina required multiple phone calls, coordinating departure times and connecting flights. It was long after midnight when she'd arrived in Greenbrae the night before, travel weary and sleep deprived.

The limousine pulled to a stop and Anne got out. The first thing she saw was the green striped awning sheltering the newly dug gravesite. On either side were rows of metal folding chairs for friends and family.

She did not recognize many people. Most were Nonie's friends of long standing. There were more friends than family, actually. Only two of Lenora Sherwood's three sons were here today to mourn her.

Anne's father, Chandler, a navy pilot, had been killed when she was only three. She had no real memory of him, except for the photograph of a young man in uniform in a silver frame on her bureau.

The Sherwood men were all extremely good-looking. She glanced at Uncle Curtis, deeply tanned, youthful, hair sun-bleached almost white. What was it he told her he did? Oh, yes. He ran a party-fishing boat for tourists in Florida. In contrast, Uncle Randall, Lesley's father, dignified in his dark blue suit, looked every inch the conservative lawyer he was, practicing in the nearby town of Larchmont.

Lesley stood between him and her mother, Aunt Adele. Wearing her pale blond hair pulled back by a contrasting black velvet hairband that matched the black sheath she wore, Lesley looked fragile. Much changed from the plump teenager Anne remembered, Lesley was now a slender young woman. Too slender? Anne's mother, Brenda, who ran a modeling agency in Beverly Hills, wouldn't agree. Her comment would be, "A perfect size three!"

Uncle Randall motioned them forward to take their places in the row of seats reserved for the immediate family. Nonie's minister had arrived wearing his starched surplice and flowing cassock, and was advancing with his prayer book in hand.

"I hope he'll make it short," Bret murmured to Anne as they sat down. "Nonie would have hated a long-winded eulogy."

As Reverend Anson began to speak, Bret slipped on her dark glasses and gritted her teeth. Her head was throbbing. Earlier she'd had some doubts she'd even make it to the funeral. Bret looked over at Bernessa, sitting in the opposite row. Her expression was composed, her mouth set firmly in the rich mahogany face, the dark eyes deeply sad. Bret sent her a silent message: *I owe you, Bernessa.*

The night before, still in shock from the news of Nonie's death, Bret had fortified herself at the Atlanta airport lounge before boarding the plane. She'd had two more drinks during the bumpy trip on the commuter flight to Greenbrae. By the time she reached the Sherwood house, dazed and bleary-eyed, Bret had fallen into a heavy sleep.

That morning she woke up with a terrible hangover. Shaky and queasy, she went downstairs in search of coffee. When she stumbled into the kitchen, Bernessa, who was at the stove turning pancakes, gave Bret a sharp look. Then, without a word she mixed a lemony hot toddy and guided it into Bret's trembling hands. A large mug of strong coffee followed. By the time they left for the church, Bret felt steadier.

As she tried to concentrate on the minister's words, Bret's gaze slid over to her father. Her stomach knotted in the familiar anger. What kind of life was he living now? He seemed fit and trim, and yet his features seemed blurred, there was a sag to the chin, the flesh under the eyes looked a little puffy.

Did he feel any remorse for walking out on her and her mother? Probably not. If he did, he'd shown not a sign of it when he greeted her this morning. After the divorce, he had remarried, not once but twice. But then, so had her mother. They both seemed to have moved on without any scars. It was Bret who had been the wounded one.

Bret looked away. In spite of the tranquilizer she

had gulped right before they left for church, her nerves felt raw. Wouldn't this ever be over? She couldn't take much more.

Lesley clasped her hands together tensely, feeling the ridge of her engagement ring under her gloves. A familiar panic swept over her. She took a sudden deep breath. Immediately she was aware of her mother's anxious glance. Like a tape running in her head Lesley heard her mother's voice from that morning insisting, "But, darling, you really must eat something. The service may be long, then the ride out to the cemetery for the graveside ceremony. Just coffee's not enough." And her own quiet reply: "I'm fine. Please don't fuss."

It was the same pattern over and over between them. Adele pleading, Lesley resisting quietly but inwardly enraged, screaming silently, *I'm not a child! I'll eat what I want when I want it. It's my body. It's my life!*

Sun glinted on the edge of the silver-toned coffin, sending off a glare of blinding light. All at once Lesley felt faint. Her mother had been right. The service had been overly long, the church crowded, airless, heavy with the fragrance of flowers. She felt vaguely nauseated. Discreetly she opened her handbag and took out a small box of no-calorie mints and slipped one into her mouth.

To divert her mind, Lesley turned her attention on Anne. How serene she looked, and poised. There was something demure, almost Victorian, about Anne; the soft gray knit suit, the gray silk blouse with a bow at the throat. Her hair, gleaming like polished maple in the afternoon sunshine, was drawn smoothly back from her face and fastened at the nape of her neck with a tortoise-shell barrette. She looked so at peace with herself. *I wish I had that—whatever it is…* Lesley's thought was left unfinished because people were standing for Reverend Anson's last blessing.

"Surely goodness and mercy shall follow me, all the days of my life, And I will dwell in the house of the Lord forever."

Lesley steadied herself against a wave of dizziness. The minister was coming down the line of family members, shaking hands, offering condolences. Rigidly she awaited her turn.

Then, people started moving toward the cars parked on the road below the sloping lawn.

Everyone was departing, leaving Nonie alone here on the hillside. Lesley's throat tightened. She would have liked to stay, to say her goodbye to Nonie alone. But her father's hand was on her arm. "Come along, dear."

An hour later they were all gathered at Nonie's rambling clapboard and fieldstone house, known in Greenbrae as "the old Sherwood place." Built in 1850, it had been lived in by generations of Sherwoods. The friends and neighbors who had come offering sympathy and comforting words were gone now. Only the family remained.

When they were all assembled in the living room Bernessa brought in a tray carrying a silver coffee urn and a platter of sandwiches. After they had shared the light meal, Uncle Randall began to address them.

"May I have your attention for a few minutes?" he began in a lawyerly tone. "While we're all still together, I think it would be a good time to discuss Mother's will. It won't be probated for another few weeks. However, since one of the provisions directly concerns you three young ladies, I felt I should bring this to your attention before you each go back to your own lives.''

He looked at his brother.

''No offense to you, Curtis. It's just that since I was nearby and also a lawyer with the firm that handled Mother's affairs, it was only natural that she should consult with me about some of the specifics. As you will find, everything is in good order, and with her infinite sense of fairness Mother divided everything equally between you, me and Chandler's widow.'' Randall cleared his throat and continued, ''However, Mother was very definite about what she wanted to do with the beach cottage at Sea Watch Cove. She has left it jointly to the three of you.'' Randall looked directly at Anne, Bret and Lesley. ''Her granddaughters.''

Anne was stunned.

''Spindrift?'' Lesley was the first to find her voice.

''To *us?*'' gasped Bret.

''Yes,'' Randall affirmed. ''But with certain conditions.''

Chapter Two

Later that night the three cousins gathered in Nonie's old-fashioned kitchen.

Anne stood at the stove stirring the milk she was heating in the hope that the hot drink before bedtime would ease her into a good night's sleep.

Bret, perched on a stool at the counter, sipped the nightcap she had made for herself and said, "I still don't understand why Nonie left Spindrift to us."

"Well, Dad said it was outlined pretty clearly in the will," Lesley answered. "During the next year we are each to spend a week here alone, then—at the end of the summer—meet together and decide whether to keep the cottage, rent it during the season or sell it and split the profits."

A silence fell among them as each one pondered this unexpected legacy. Anne turned off the burner and carefully poured her steaming milk into a mug and brought it over to the counter.

"Do you realize it's been ten years since we were all together at Spindrift?" Lesley looked at the others.

Anne nodded. "I can hardly believe it's been that long."

"I don't know about you two, but I feel every one of these past ten years," Bret said, looking at Lesley. "Of course, you don't look a day over seventeen, Les, which is about what you were the last time I saw you. Teaching kindergarten must be the fountain of youth." Then she turned her gaze on Anne. "And *you*, leading a secluded life behind the ivy-covered walls of a college."

"I wouldn't exactly describe it like that, Bret."

"Well, however you describe it, it must be a less stressful life than mine."

"Yours sounds so glamorous, Bret!" Lesley exclaimed. "Traveling all over, staying at wonderful hotels, resorts—"

"Glamorous? No way," Bret scoffed. "Being a rep for a costume jewelry firm is anything but. I practically live in airports, out of a suitcase. Everything begins to seem the same. Waking up in a hotel room that looks just like the one you were in the night before, only in a different city. Sometimes having to call the switchboard operator to find out exactly where you are—Dallas, Atlanta, New Orleans." She swirled her drink. "I think that's what's aging me."

"*Aging* you!" the other two exclaimed derisively.

"I'm twenty-seven and feel forty."

"You're less than a year older than I am," protested Lesley.

"And I'm only six months older," Anne reminded her.

"Well, we're all too near the big three-oh for comfort," Bret said firmly.

"Speak for yourself, Bret." Anne laughed. "Some

people say a woman doesn't even begin to get interesting until she's thirty."

"That may be some comfort to you, but look at the statistics. There's not much hope for a single woman born after 1970."

"Hope for what?" Lesley frowned.

"To find the proverbial Mr. Right—love, marriage, the picket fence and all that." Bret halted, then looked pointedly at Lesley. "Of course, we don't have to worry about *you*. Who could miss that rock on your left hand. Who's the lucky guy?"

Lesley looked slightly embarrassed. "His name's Van Madison."

"When's the wedding?"

"We haven't set the date yet. Van's studying for his bar exam, so I'm not sure—"

"Not sure of the date or not sure, period?" Bret raised her eyebrows.

Lesley gave a wan smile, got up from the kitchen stool, opened the top of the trash can and dumped in her orange peelings. "As soon as *I* know, I'll let *you* know, Bret."

"Don't forget, we all promised to be in each other's weddings."

Lesley wiped her hands daintily on a small kitchen towel, announcing, "I'm going to call it a night. Think we can get an early start tomorrow?"

Since they all had planes to catch and jobs to return to, they had decided to drive down to Sea Watch Cove for the weekend and view their inheritance.

After Lesley left, Bret topped off her drink. Anne felt tired, but she didn't want to leave her cousin alone. She poured the rest of the warm milk into her mug, then rinsed out the saucepan and put it in the drainer.

"Come on, Anne, tell me about your life in the north woods," Bret teased.

"It's hardly the north woods, Bret. You'd be surprised. Glenharbor is a sophisticated California community, and my work in Public Relations is very interesting. The college is a very progressive one, and so there's always something going on at the campus. Not dull at all—we get lots of big-time celebrities in all the arts, and there are concerts, receptions, book signings as well as local artists and writers. Believe it or not, I thoroughly enjoy my job and my life."

Bret tilted her head to one side, surveying Anne curiously. "What about men? Or are they all staid professors, intellectuals?"

"Some are, but not all," Anne replied, thinking of Dale Myers. But she wasn't about to talk about him, especially not with Bret. Determined to change the subject from herself, Anne went on, "I was surprised to hear you tell Aunt Adele you gave up the boutique."

"Got fed up with the hassle. Filling out tax forms, placating picky customers, going to trade shows, always trying to anticipate what people might want a year in advance."

"And being a jewelry rep is better?"

"Less responsibility. The sales figures don't depend completely on you, but on the popularity of the current design you're presenting. Anyway, it suits me for now. Who knows for how long?" Then Bret asked bluntly, "Why didn't you stay in Southern California and work with your mother, Anne?"

"Talk about a stressful career!" Anne rolled her

eyes. "The pace is incredible—I don't see how my mother does it. *I* sure wouldn't want it."

"With your looks, Anne, *you* could have been a model. Didn't you ever think of it? I bet your mother did."

Anne winced mentally. Bret could have taped Brenda's old argument. "Thanks for the compliment, Bret, if that's what it was. The short answer is, I couldn't stand always being concerned about how I look, the tiniest flaw, wrinkle, pound. That's what a professional model's life is like, and it's definitely not for me." She stifled a yawn. "Enough of this inquisition. It's getting late. I'm off to bed, Bret. How about you?"

At noon the next day they left Greenbrae for Sea Watch Cove in Lesley's car. They were silent as Lesley maneuvered through the expressway traffic, heavier than usual because it was Friday and people were escaping town for the weekend.

They swung off the expressway onto an access road, and from there started down a two-lane highway leading to the ocean. Through the open car windows they could smell the unique combination of piney woods and sea peculiar to this North Carolina coastal area.

A little farther along they saw the sign, and all three read it out loud—"Sea Watch Cove"—then burst out laughing.

"Almost there," announced Lesley.

They rounded a bend at the crest of a little rise and Lesley slowed the car. "Oh, look!" she exclaimed, pointing to a brilliant blue rim of ocean sparkling in the sun. Foamy lace swirls formed on the crescent-shaped beach with each breaking wave.

Lesley made the turn off the main road onto a rutted one leading downhill to a cluster of buildings; a gas station, a post office and grocery store, a café and a few small stores, most of them boarded up and posted with signs that read Closed till May 30.

"Looks exactly the same," Bret said. "Nothing's changed."

"We need to get some groceries," Anne told them. "Bernessa said there'd be staples but nothing fresh. She said Nonie stayed down later this year—after Labor Day—because the weather was so nice. She planned to come back and stay longer."

"Bernessa said she seemed just fine when they got to Greenbrae, but said she felt a little tired and was going to lie down for a while...."

"Then just went to sleep." Anne finished quietly.

"Well, thank goodness she went that way! No lingering illness, no pain," Bret said briskly. "I couldn't stand to think of Nonie suffering."

Lesley pulled into a parking place in front of Dennison's Giant Superette.

"I'm amazed it's still standing." Bret said, as she got out of the car and gestured to the weatherbeaten wooden building.

"I thought it might have washed away by now," Anne remarked as they went up the sagging steps.

Inside, the superette was dark and dingy. A clerk sat behind the cash register reading a comic book and drinking a can of cola. He barely looked up as they walked in, then went back to his reading.

They found a rickety-wheeled wire basket that creaked and veered slightly as they pushed it down one aisle and up another. Each began putting in various items at random.

"Remember, we're only going to be here until Sunday," cautioned Anne, pausing to decide between a can of pineapple chunks or applesauce.

"That's right. We don't want to get a lot of stuff we won't eat." Lesley put a box of crackers back on the shelf. "I guess that's it."

"Whoa, aren't we going to get some vino?" Bret demanded. The other two didn't say anything, so she went on, "This is a special occasion, right? Our ten-year reunion?"

"Sure, I guess so." Lesley looked at Anne. "What kind? I don't know anything about wine. What do you suggest?"

"Just because I live in California doesn't mean I'm an expert on wine!" Anne laughed. "I think there's a rule of thumb—fish and poultry go with white; steak—or, in our case, hamburger—goes with red."

"Why not a bottle of both?" Bret walked up the aisle to the liquor department, brought back two bottles and put them in the cart.

The clerk unwound himself from the high stool and indifferently rang up the groceries. They each took a bag and went out the door. Lesley unlocked the trunk, and they stashed the bags inside.

Bret halted at the top of the store steps. "Wait a minute, I forgot something," she called to her cousins, then turned and went back into the store. A few minutes later she emerged with another small bag and hopped into the back seat.

Anne noticed the top of another wine bottle sticking out the top of Bret's bag. She felt a stirring of uneasiness but dismissed it. Bret was an adult. She could certainly do what she wanted without Anne's approval.

Lesley backed the car out and shifted into low gear as they went down a bumpy, sandy road. Most of the windows of the cottages along the way were boarded.

Almost at the end of the road, Lesley braked. She had to shift into reverse and swing sharply around to turn into the carport behind the slant-roofed, sea-silvered shingled cottage.

Without a word the three women got out of the car. The air was brine scented, and they drew long breaths as if hungry for the familiar smell of it. Spindrift, at last.

They went up the wooden walkway to the screened-in porch that encircled the front of the house. Lesley got out the key her father had given her and inserted it into the lock and eased the door open. It squeaked a little on its hinges. On the threshold all three women hesitated as if none wanted to be the first to enter. It was the first time any of them had come to Spindrift without Nonie there to welcome them.

Chapter Three

That night they found candles and set the table as they remembered Nonie had always done on special occasions. The conversation took a nostalgic turn.

"I'll always remember that last summer we were all here together," Anne said wistfully.

Bret frowned. "I wonder what was the real reason Nonie left Spindrift to us."

"Probably just because she loved us and knew we had spent some of the happiest days of our lives here," Anne said. "Isn't that reason enough?"

"Those *were* the happiest days of my life. The only taste of family life I ever had were those summers with Nonie." Bret pulled a pitiful face. "I was a poor little girl from a broken home."

"No more than I was, Bret," Anne reminded her. "My father died before I could even remember him, and my mother— Well, Brenda was so involved in her work." Anne did not say *her men,* but she remembered the sun-bronzed young male models with narrow hips, broad shoulders and long muscular legs who had passed through the agency doors. Brenda had taken a special interest in several of them while promoting their careers.

"I loved coming here, too," Lesley said. "I hated when my parents bought the summer place in the mountains and I had to go up there with them on my college vacations. I missed coming to Spindrift. Those summers were special."

When they had cleared the table, then washed and put away the dinner dishes, they continued chatting but on a less serious level. It was Lesley who at last ended the evening. "I'm sorry to break this up, but I can hardly keep my eyes open."

"Me, too," Anne said getting up, stretching. "Where are we all sleeping?"

"I'm bunking down here on the studio couch," Bret told them. "I should warn you both that I'm an insomniac. I get up and prowl at night, so if you want a sound night's sleep, you'd better bed down at a safe distance."

"I'll sleep in the loft." Lesley headed to the stairway that led to a large room on the second floor. That had been their sleeping quarters in the old days— three cots placed under the eaves facing the small dormer windows that looked out onto the beach. Long after their bedtime the cousins would stay awake whispering secrets, telling stories, making plans.

Anne opted to sleep in Nonie's former bedroom.

After the others had gone, Bret took the bottle of wine left from dinner, filled her glass, then stretched out on the lumpy sofa bed. Alone in the front room, with the windows open on the ocean side, she heard the pounding of the surf. The sound brought back a rush of memories from all those long-ago summers.

This cottage held so much of her almost forgotten self.

She had found the evening troubling. They had not been able to recapture the closeness they had once had. Even with the effort they had all made to talk of past adventures and funny incidents, the reunion hadn't worked. And bringing up that last summer spent here together had been a mistake. She had forgotten some of the teenage tensions, the conflicts, clashes of temper. Ten years, for Pete's sake. They had all grown into different people.

In spite of the candlelight, the wine, the intimacy of being alone at Spindrift, they were still strangers. What had Nonie hoped to accomplish by bringing them here together again?

Bret drained her wineglass and pulled one of Nonie's afghans over her shoulders. She didn't remember falling asleep.

The sound of movement in the kitchen just off the living room woke her up. Bret raised herself up on her elbows, squinting heavy-lidded eyes at the bright sunlight pouring in through the windows. The smell of coffee wafted tantalizingly and she called, "Will somebody be an angel and pour me a cup?"

Anne appeared, bringing a steaming mug. "The weather is glorious. I suggest we take a picnic and spend the day at the beach."

Bret needed another mug of the strong black coffee before she could get moving. The other two packed a wicker hamper and headed down to the beach.

"I'll be down in a while," she promised.

Anne and Lesley found a sheltered place behind the dunes. Anne unfolded the small canvas lounge chair, sat down and adjusted her wide-brimmed straw hat, sighing contentedly. "Isn't this great? The sun feels marvelous. The beaches in Northern California are not very conducive to sunbathing."

Lesley spread out a blanket, unzipped her terry cover-up and lay down. "Yes, it's wonderful," she murmured as she stretched out. "I may just drift off, Anne. Don't think I'm being rude. It's just that I didn't sleep very well last night for some reason. Maybe the surf pounding. I guess I'm not used to it."

"Sure, I understand. I'm going to relax myself." Anne glanced at her cousin. In her swimsuit Lesley looked almost skeletal, far thinner than Anne remembered her—a fact Bret had tactlessly remarked on last night. They were looking at some of Nonie's old photo albums, laughing at their own past images. Anne had pointed to her own metallic smile one summer. "Well, at least, I don't have my braces anymore."

"Yeah," Bret added, "and Lesley is skinny now."

Lesley had reacted snappily. "Don't remind me how disgustingly fat I was!"

Seeing that Lesley was really upset, Anne had hastened to say, "Not fat, Les. Nonie always said 'pleasantly plump.'"

"That made it even worse." Lesley sighed. "I knew she was just being kind. Nonie would never say anything hurtful."

But it wasn't only in appearance that they had all changed.

Bret's transformation was even more puzzling. There was a hard edge to her now that she'd lacked at seventeen. Sure, she had been volatile and quicktempered, but also generous and warmhearted, uncritical.

Anne shifted her position, rubbed some sunblock on her arms and again thought about her cousins. The fact that they were so different shouldn't be surprising, given that they had all grown up in different parts of the country, in different environments.

Yes, they had all changed; everything had—everything but Spindrift itself. Their grandmother's cottage was the same. It had the same wonderful, embracing warmth Anne remembered from her childhood.

The surprise inheritance of Spindrift was the thing that occupied Anne's thoughts most. Her premonition that the weekend at Spindrift wasn't such a good idea had not been borne out. For the three of them, who had once been so close, shared secrets, confidences, been more than sisters to each other during those summers…the camaraderie had been forced. They were, after all, strangers.

Lesley wasn't really sleepy; she just didn't want to talk. Lying on her stomach, she rested her chin on her arms and stared out at the ocean. Layers of colors for miles and miles. There must be at least ten shades of blue. She felt the sun needle into her back, her eyes begin to sting, and she slipped on dark glasses.

Coming back to Spindrift had had an unexpected effect. She felt depressed. All sorts of things had come rushing back. Things she had tried to forget but couldn't. She had not forgotten Craig, nor would she ever forget him. She should have by now. It had been ten years. She should be thinking of Van. She was going to marry him. Or at least she had said she would.

Unconsciously, Lesley twisted the engagement ring on her finger. She shouldn't have taken it. But Van had given it to her in front of everybody at her parents' Christmas Eve party. Lesley suppressed an involuntary shiver, remembering....

In Larchmont, twenty-eight-year-old Van Madison, was considered one of the town's most eligible bachelors, with his good looks, easy charm and future potential.

He was fourth-generation Larchmont, but although his family was long on pedigree, they were short on money. Still, he had attended Crossfields, the prestigious prep school for boys where senators, top-ranking military men and millionaires sent their sons. From there he had gone to Davidson and on to Harvard Law School. Van not only belonged in the best circles of Larchmont society, he epitomized for everyone else what it took to belong.

At first Lesley had been flattered by Van's attention. She had never outgrown her self-image of being the chubby, plain little girl—the last one chosen at dancing class parties.

Lesley had told herself she didn't care to go to parties, that she'd rather stay home, read a book, listen to her records or watch TV. It was her mother, Adele, who agonized over this. Adele had been a typical Southern belle and had dreamed her daughter would enjoy the same kind of youthful popularity. The problem was that her daughter was unwilling to play the role in which her mother had cast her.

Adele had been thrilled by Lesley's engagement to Van. Now she was happily planning their wedding. Slick-covered *Bride's* magazines addressed to Lesley kept arriving at the house, filled with ads for linens, silver, china and housewares.

Only a few weeks ago, when Lesley seemed indifferent to her mother's enthusiastic talk about silver patterns and styles of invitations, Adele had thrown up her hands. "What is the matter with you? Don't you care?"

Lesley had hastened to reassure her mother. But the truth was, she didn't care about the huge, extravagant wedding her mother seemed to think appropriate just to impress her relatives and friends.

Lesley grabbed a handful of sand, letting it drift through her fingers. *I should be able to have the kind of wedding I want—that is, if I want a wedding at all! I should marry the man I want. Do I really want to marry Van?* Her question begged an answer, and of its own volition one came: *Free! I want to be free! To make my own choices, make my own decisions, to live my own life!*

Was that possible?

Just then Bret joined them. "Hello, you two."

Anne raised her head and gave a little wave. "What took you so long?"

Bret set down a small plastic cooler. "Went to the store for some reinforcements for our libation," she replied jauntily, opening the top of the cooler and pulling up a bottle of wine. "Anyone want to join me?"

Anne put her head back down, declining drowsily, "No, thanks."

"Les?" Bret asked.

"I think I'll wait on that." Lesley, too, sounded sleepy.

Taking out one of the wineglasses she had stuck, stem up, into the ice in the small chest, Bret opened the bottle and poured herself a glass.

For Bret this weekend had stirred up some of the

old envy she was ashamed of but had to admit. Both of her cousins had seemed to have so much more security, so many more opportunities, than she. Lesley had always had the picture-perfect life, with affluent parents who adored her. While she, Bret, had—what? Her bitter parents playing Ping-Pong with her. Not knowing from one part of the year to the other where she would be or with which parent, which stepparent she'd have to try to get along with. Only the summers were secure...with Nonie. And that last summer she'd almost managed to wreck even that safe haven.

It all started to come back. The dune grass bent in the sea wind and the smell of the salty air made pictures spring instantly to life in her mind. The sound of laughter, transistor music, young toast-tan bodies in the barest briefs and bikinis, the thunk of a volleyball, the taste of "Purple Lightning"—a vodka-and-grape-juice concoction someone had brought in a plastic half-gallon jug. Her first taste of alcohol.

Then, at night, sitting around fires built of driftwood, smoking up into starlight, or huddled in college-labeled sweatshirts waiting for a slow moon to rise over the dark rippling ocean. Then, later still, couples pairing off...

Bret yanked herself back to the present, away from the bittersweet memories. She had been such a fool.

It was too late to think about all that now. It had happened, and that summer was over. Long over. Still, the memory of that last weekend flashed like an exploding Roman candle in her brain. All that she wished had never happened. In spite of the sun's heat, Bret shuddered.

Bret felt the familiar loneliness sweep over her. She

remembered the look on Nonie's face when she'd crept into the cottage just as dawn was breaking. Bret suppressed a groan at the memory.

Lesley got up languidly. "Think I'll go take a dip. Want to come?"

"No, not just now." Bret looked at her. In her skimpy pink bikini Lesley looked about twelve. Watching her departing figure, Bret frowned, glanced at Anne. "My gosh, Les is thin—too thin, don't you think?"

When there was no answer, Bret realized her cousin was asleep. Good conscience, she thought ironically. Anne was always so composed. She had never seemed to go through an awkward age, at least not during their summers at Spindrift. Bret's gaze rested on Anne's head, the mellow-gold of her hair, now twisted up from her neck in a loose knot, glinting in the sun. Anne had never had those ups and downs she herself had gone through in adolescence, usually about some boy or another. No, Anne moved in a kind of unaffected aloofness. Bret couldn't remember how many times, during those summers they spent at Spindrift, some guy she herself had been interested in had asked, "How about fixing me up with your cousin from California?" But Anne was never interested.

Anne's cool detachment wasn't the only thing about her that Bret envied. She was also jealous of Anne because Bret suspected Anne was Nonie's favorite. Not that Nonie ever showed any one of them more affection than the other. Still the thought had persisted, rankling in Bret. Once in a fit of temper she had actually accused Nonie of favoring her cousin.

When Nonie explained that Anne had grown up without a father and so needed lots of extra love, Bret protested, "So do I!" Nonie had just laughed and hugged her.

And I still do! Bret cried silently, pouring the last of the wine into her glass. If only, she thought ruefully, she hadn't opened so many wrong doors looking for it.

Part II

Chapter Four

After collecting her suitcase at the baggage carousel, Anne caught a cab from the airport to Beverly Hills.

When she'd called to tell her mother about Nonie's death, Brenda had urged, "On your return flight, come through L.A. instead of San Francisco. That way we can have a nice visit. It's been months since I've seen you."

Anne had agreed to the suggestion but was now having second thoughts. As had been the case on other visits, Brenda might not be all that available. There was always something demanding her attention—an upcoming fashion show, a photo shoot, a new class of models to train. Still, she *had* promised…

The cab came to a stop at a driveway illuminated by tiki lights going up a stunted-palm-tree-lined drive to a Spanish-style house. A discreet sign on the porch pillars identified it as the Brenda Sherwood Agency.

Anne paid the driver, got out and, carrying her

bags, went up the steps to the carved oak door with its wrought-iron-grilled amber glass half window.

A few minutes after ringing the doorbell, Anne heard the tap of high heels on the tiled floor and saw through the glass the figure of her mother approaching.

"Darling! You're here!" Brenda exclaimed and leaned forward to place an incredibly smooth cheek against hers, enveloping Anne in her aura of jasmine scent. "Come in, come in."

Once Anne was inside, Brenda's gaze moved swiftly over her daughter, noting everything she was wearing. Anne knew the look and half expected some comment but it did not come.

"Welcome home."

Home was the agency; the agency was home. Both were designed to create an ambiance that was completely and uniquely hers. Everything was black and white: the tile floors, the walls and furniture, the rugs and lamps. Black and white, the perfect background for Brenda's blond beauty.

"How are you, darling? Was the flight dreadfully long and tiresome? Air travel used to be fun. Now they pack you in like sardines. Did you have anything to eat or are you famished?"

While Brenda talked, she relieved Anne of her tote bag and suitcase and placed both at the bottom of a winding staircase with scrolled black iron railings.

As she watched Brenda's graceful movements, Anne had the same astonished realization of just how beautiful her mother was that she had every time she saw her.

Brenda Bales had arrived in California from a small town in Idaho in the late fifties. She'd had some vague aspirations to movie stardom, but when she saw the heartbreak and downfall of many of her peers, Brenda had settled for modeling.

Hired by an exclusive women's specialty shop, she often modeled in the restaurants of posh Beverly Hills hotels during fund-raisers for various charities. It was at one of these events that she had been introduced to Chandler Sherwood, Anne's father, who was training to become a navy pilot and was stationed in San Diego. Theirs had been a whirlwind romance. There had hardly been time to notify their relatives when an air accident had ended their brief marriage leaving Brenda pregnant with Anne. Brenda had no desire to travel to North Carolina to meet his family. Instead she decided to make a career of something she knew—modeling. On the proverbial shoestring, her small widow's pension, and her own determination and ability, she had established the Brenda Sherwood Agency.

Lenora Sherwood, her husband's mother, was the only one of the Sherwood family who kept in touch. Through the years she had sent birthday and Christmas gifts to her granddaughter. It was when Anne was nine that the most interesting and lasting gift had come. Lenora had invited the little girl to come to North Carolina to spend the summer at her beach cottage, Spindrift. In her letter she had written, "Bretnay and Lesley, the daughters of Chandler's brothers, Randall and Curtis, are nearly the same age and will be coming, too. It would be wonderful for Anne to get to know her cousins. If you give permission for her to come, I promise I will take the greatest care of your daughter and I assure you that I am eager to have her. With fondest regards…'' She had enclosed a check for airfare and travel expenses.

The invitation could not have come at a better time. Brenda had taken on her biggest project yet—a bridal show for a Rodeo Drive boutique specializing in wedding dresses, accessories and bridesmaids gowns. To have Anne out of the way and taken care of for weeks was an answer to all her problems.

So Anne went and thus began the tradition of her and Bret and Lesley spending every summer for the next eight years with Nonie at Spindrift.

Coming out of her reverie, Anne realized her mother was beckoning her down the hall.

''Come along, darling, there's someone I want you to meet,'' Brenda said over her shoulder as she led the way along the hall then down two steps into the white-carpeted living room.

At their entrance a tall man with a lean, handsome face and a shock of iron-gray hair languidly unfolded himself from one of the deep white velour armchairs. He looked vaguely familiar. Had she seen him in a TV commercial?

''Tony, this is my daughter, Anne.''

''Anne, Tony Abbot. He's my new business consultant.''

Tony smiled at Anne appreciatively, then turned back to Brenda. ''How is it Anne's not one of your top models, Bren?''

Brenda shrugged. ''Don't ask me, Tony. I tried, but Anne was never interested.''

''Can I fix you a drink, Anne?'' Tony asked casually, starting toward the built-in bar against the wall.

She shook her head. ''No, thanks.'' She turned to

Brenda. "Actually, Mom, if it's okay, I think I'll excuse myself. I'm awfully tired, jet lag, probably."

"Well, all right, dear. We'll have plenty of time to catch up on things tomorrow."

Brenda walked out to the hall with her. "I've put you in the small room off the sewing room. We've been using your regular bedroom for an extra fitting room. I hope you don't mind."

"No, not at all." Anne hadn't actually had a "regular" room here since college.

"You'll feel better after a good night's sleep." Brenda kissed her cheek. "Sweet dreams, dear."

Anne closed the door and leaned against it for a minute. She wouldn't be missed downstairs.

Anne walked over to the window. All the rooms on this side of the house overlooked the patio and the lighted swimming pool. A pool with fake rock and lush ferns where no one swam. It was only used for publicity stills of slender nymphs in bikinis whose moussed hair wouldn't survive a drop of water and tanned glistening young men flexing their muscles hoping for a sun lotion ad or commercial.

Tony's question about her mother's failure to employ her rankled. It brought back all the arguments with her mother over the years.

In spite of Brenda's insistence that she would make a great model, Anne had never wanted to call attention to herself. Especially not after what had happened when she was fourteen.

Anne shuddered, remembering. As a member of her high school swim team she had planned to do some practice laps one Saturday. She had come out to the pool not knowing a photo shoot was scheduled. She hadn't seen Rod stretched out on one of the lounges. Rod McKenna, one of Brenda's top models, had been on the cover of *GQ, Sports Illustrated, Ski* and a number of other magazines. Wearing a regulation tank suit, Anne was poised on the diving board ready to go in, when she heard a long, low whistle.

Startled, she had turned to see Rod unfold himself and come to the edge of the pool. Her heart began to pound. She had only two choices: turn and leave or complete her dive and swim to the end of the pool. She made a quick racing dive and swam to the other end. When she surfaced, Rod was blocking her way up the ladder. He grinned down at her.

A feeling of panic had swept over Anne. She felt trapped. Frightened. Of what she wasn't sure. There had been something menacing in Rod's narrowed eyes. If her mother and the photographer had not come out on the patio just then, she feared what might have happened.

Anne had never told Brenda about the incident. It would have sounded foolish, exaggerated. But after that, Anne avoided the pool area during the week when the models were in and out of the office checking their assignment schedules.

She had also become self-consciously aware of her newly developed figure. That realization marked the beginning of her deliberately hiding her curves, wearing oversize sweaters, shapeless men's shirts, eschewing makeup and pulling her hair straight back in a ponytail—much to Brenda's despair.

Anne concentrated on her schoolwork, working for high grades, never dating. When she graduated from college, Brenda had tried again to draw her daughter into her agency, if not as a model, then as part of the business end.

"With your organizational skills I could devote more time to what I do best."

But Anne was adamant. She still wanted nothing to do with modeling or models. She had already applied for the public-relations job at Glenharbor with every intention of accepting the anticipated offer. "Mom, I'm not interested in the business. I want a different kind of life."

"Burying yourself in a second-rate college in an out-of-the-way town somewhere up north doesn't sound like much of a life." Brenda pouted.

"It's what I want, Mom. I'm sorry to disappoint you."

Brenda was disappointed. She kept pointing out that she had spent a small fortune on Anne's education, believing it would pay off in a partnership that would strengthen the business she had struggled so long to build. But in the end she had to acknowledge that—along with some other, admirable traits—her daughter had inherited her own stubbornness.

"Sweet dreams," Brenda had said tonight, just as she always had throughout Anne's life.

This was a house of dreams. Brenda had made her dream come true. The young people who walked through the agency door had dreams, ones based on shallow hopes of success and fame. Unrealistic dreams. Or were they any more unrealistic than Anne's own dreams? A husband, a home, children, love—enduring love that lasted forever. And was it too late for her to find them?

Impeccably dressed and perfectly made up, Brenda was in the black-and-white kitchen on the white phone. She mouthed a silent "Good morning" to Anne and went on talking.

Anne poured herself a cup of coffee. Only half listening to her mother's side of the conversation, she scanned the headlines of the morning paper lying on the counter.

When Brenda hung up, a small frown puckered her smooth forehead as she wrote something in her appointment book, then asked, "What time is your flight?"

"Six-something to San Francisco. My plane up the coast leaves at eight."

Brenda pursed her lips. "Oh, darling, I won't be able to drive you to the airport, I'm afraid."

"I understand, Mom. Please don't worry. I can get to the airport fine."

Anne slid onto one of the black leather stools at the black-and-white marble counter.

"I really am sorry, darling. I have to go." Brenda emptied her coffee into the sink. "I've provided several of my models to pretty up the scenery at this gala, and I have to be there to see that everything goes smoothly. That no one does anything foolish." She rolled her blue eyes dramatically. "It's like being chaperon at the junior prom. Some of the girls are all beauty and no brains. I have to guide them. You understand, don't you?"

How well she understood, Anne thought wryly.

"Of course." Anne took a sip of coffee. "Don't worry about me."

"This isn't working out to be much of a visit, darling, is it? I haven't even heard all about your grandmother's funeral, the gathering of the clan and your time with your cousins. Was it dreadful?"

"Not at all. The service was lovely in its way."
Anne told her about the funeral, the family and especially her cousins.

"Are the girls married?" was Brenda's next
question.

"No, but Lesley is engaged. I don't know much
about Bret's life. We were just together for the two
days at Spindrift. Not time enough for any deep discussions or in-depth confidences." Anne paused.
"The big surprise was that Nonie left Spindrift to the
three of us."

"Is that good, or did you inherit a white elephant?"

"I'm not sure what you mean."

"I mean beachfront property here in California is
like a gold mine. I don't know if back East it's a
liability. You read all these horror stories about the
dunes eroding and beaches shrinking from hurricanes.
I just wondered if the property's a liability, with taxes
and all. Nonie had the cottage forever, and I wondered if it's been kept up."

"It's in perfect condition, Mom. And from what
Uncle Randall told us, taxes and everything are paid
through next year, when we're to make up our minds
about what to do with it."

"Surely you don't intend to keep it! I mean, what
would you do with it three thousand miles away. If
prices are good, why not sell? Even at one third of
the purchase price, you could make a nice bundle.
Maybe take a cruise or go to Europe. You have any
number of exciting options." She took a long breath.
"Please do get away from that backwoods college
and the isolated environment you've chosen to bury
yourself in."

Trying not to sound condescending, Anne said patiently, "Mom, if you'd come up to visit me, you would see for yourself that it isn't a cultural wasteland. It's a thriving, interesting community filled with creative people with ideas and fascinating careers."

"Oh, well, I realize I can't say anything to change your mind, Anne. I just wish you'd take advantage of some of my connections here in L.A. and at least *try* living with me for a while."

Both the breakfast and their conversation finished, Brenda put things in the dishwasher. "I have to get ready to drive to Malibu for this affair, but I feel guilty leaving you alone on your only day here."

"Don't worry, Mom. No problem. I understand."

"You always were incredibly generous, Anne. I seem to be forever running out on you. I really am sorry. You sure you don't mind, then?"

"It's okay, Mom, I told you."

Anne got up and went over to her mother. She gave her a careful hug, not wanting to disturb the hairdo, the makeup.

"It's been lovely having you here, darling. Call me when you get in and keep in touch, won't you?"

"Of course, Mom. Thanks for everything."

It was an easy flight of less than an hour from San Francisco. Anne had left her small car in the airport's long-term parking lot. With only a little coaxing, the engine caught and she drove the few miles along the highway to the section of the town dominated by the college and soon pulled up in front of a small Victorian house.

She sat there for a moment looking with satisfaction at the tiny house, overloaded with gingerbread on its eaves and porch. She was inordinately happy to be home. She remembered how lucky she felt to have found this little gem of a house when she had first come to Glenharbor. When she began looking for a place to live, she thought she would have to settle for a studio apartment or maybe a duplex. But a picturesque vintage house circa 1890s? It was a childhood dream come true. A dollhouse of her own to decorate, play house in. No matter that the floors tilted a little because of the slanted foundation on the eroding hillside, or that windows stuck when you tried to raise or shut them. That the fireplaces didn't work and the rooms were damp in the long rainy winters. She had fallen in love with it at first sight and was willing to overlook some of its obvious flaws. The rent was reasonable, the location idyllic. She could walk through the woodland trails to the campus and to her job.

It was entirely different from Los Angeles, from the clogged freeways and crowded streets. Anne loved it all. She remembered when her mother had asked doubtfully, "Are you sure you want to live so far away from everything?" Yet that was *exactly* what she did want.

BRET

Bret rented a car and drove back to Charlotte. Even at Spindrift she had worried about the presentations she had neglected to make the past week and all the piled-up sales reports for last month. She had a full week of customer calls and reports to fill out to make up for the week she had been gone. Then there was the trip to Atlanta next week and a conference with her supervisor, Linda Mercer, about the promotion for a new line of costume jewelry.

She shouldn't have taken the extra time off to go

to Spindrift. But it had seemed important. In light of everything that had happened this past week—Nonie's death, seeing her father, being with her cousins—her usual routine seemed unimportant. By going to Spindrift, she had hoped somehow to recapture a remnant of a past that now seemed idyllic. It hadn't worked, though.

At Spindrift Bret had felt a deep sense of hopelessness and unhappiness. Usually she managed to keep those feelings at bay, but now the sensations pressed heavily.

When had it all started? Bret remembered the question the therapist had asked her when, in a fit of despair, she had made an appointment to see her. She had been desperate and simply picked a name out of the yellow pages.

"When do you first remember feeling unhappy?" Dr. Mervin had asked in the first session.

That question had jolted Bret. When? As a five-year-old she had lain awake in bed, in her pretty room with its Mother Goose characters stenciled around the walls, her shelves of books and games, hugging her velvet teddy bear tightly to her chest, hearing the muffled sounds of two grown-ups arguing. Her mother and father. She couldn't remember how many nights like that there were before her father disappeared out of her life. Just like that. Walked out. No explanation. No real goodbye.

He did come back one afternoon to pack more of his clothes, get some of his belongings. He had halted for a few minutes in the hallway at the living room door where she and her teenage sitter were watching *Sesame Street* on TV. Bret had turned her head to look at him, and their gazes had held for a long time.

But when she had turned back to look at Big Bird flapping his wings, she heard the click of the front door closing. It was a very final sound.

After that there had been a lot of changes, a lot of moves. Her mother had remarried; Gloria's second husband Steve, was a tennis pro she had known before her divorce. Steve had been good-looking and fun. For a while. After the brief, unsuccessful marriage ended, Gloria and Bret had moved into a small apartment and Gloria had taken a real estate course. When she finished it, she became an agent for a large realty firm. Busy building her listings, at the beck and call of prospective clients, she was never home much after that. Bret, in school full-time then, joined the ranks of the latchkey kids, coming home day after day to an empty house. Those afternoons sort of blurred into her high school years, when her mother married Paul, a fellow real estate agent. After a few months they opened their own agency, which took up more of their time. Home life was nonexistent.

For a few years after her father moved out, Bret still saw him, bouncing back and forth between him and her mother. Then their relationship dwindled to birthday cards and Christmas presents. Gradually even those stopped.

"When did I first become unhappy?" Bret had repeated the psychologist's question. A better question would be, when had she last been happy.

Bret hadn't stayed with therapy. It was too painful, and it didn't help. So the question remained unanswered. When had she started being unhappy?

In high school Bret learned to fit in. She discovered she wasn't the only kid whose parents were divorced. She was sixteen by then and already practiced in burying her pain. She got along at school and managed to keep a low profile at home. Mostly Bret avoided clashes with her mother, but one day the built-in tension between them exploded. At the end of Bret's junior year she had a terrible row with her mother. She had asked for an advance on her allowance, and Gloria had lashed out furiously.

"Not a chance! Your father is late with his support money. Again! Try asking *him* for money."

The prom was coming up. Bret was desperate to shop for a dress and matching shoes. Everyone she knew already had a gown and all its accessories. All she had was a date. Tim Jarret had asked her weeks before, but like Cinderella, she had nothing to wear.

After the fight with her mother Bret made a decision, one she would later regret. She slung her shoulder pack on and took the bus across town to her father's condominium complex.

She knew where her father was living; she hadn't known he was living with someone.

It was a shock when the door was answered by a woman. She was tall, slim, tanned, blond and clad in a sleeveless bright-blue top, a multicolored batik print sarong skirt and sandals. She stared at Bret.

"Yes?" her voice was cautious, as though Bret were a census taker or a Girl Scout selling cookies.

"Hi," Bret managed to say. "Is my— Is Curtis here?"

"Not at the moment."

"Will he be here soon?"

The woman glanced at her jeweled wristwatch. "Probably not until a little after five. What did you want to see him about?"

Bret took a breath. "I'm his daughter. Can I come in and wait?"

The blonde's eyes widened. "Oh! Well, sure." She stepped back and opened the door for Bret to walk inside.

Bret glanced around. The place had creamy, thick wall-to-wall carpeting. The furniture was modern. The TV was on, some afternoon game show. Bret watched the slim figure as she moved over to the TV and turned down the volume. "I'm Francesca," she said.

Francesca. So this was the woman who had caused her parents' breakup. At least she was one of the causes. Francesca had just been a name to Bret before. Now she was a reality.

"Would you like a soda or something?" she asked Bret.

"No, thanks. I'll just wait for my father."

"Okay." Francesca stood there uncertainly, apparently as uneasy as Bret was.

Bret felt a rising panic. Would her dad be angry that she had come? She sat down gingerly on the edge of the couch.

She still remembered the growing anxiety. Finally her father arrived. What followed had been awkward. Bret mumbled her request. There was a moment's hesitation before her father pulled out his wallet, then handed her a few bills. She didn't look to see what they were. He walked her to the door, saying as she left, "Tell your mother the check is in the mail."

What a joke. Bret just nodded and ran down the outside steps, across the parking lot and back out to the street. It wasn't until she was on the bus that she counted the bills, three twenties. Maybe it would be enough to buy a decent dress and the accessories, but she wasn't sure. Maybe she wouldn't go to the prom anyway. Not if she couldn't do the whole enchilada. Maybe going to her dad had been another mistake.

Another stupid mistake. One of many, Bret thought, pounding her fist on the steering wheel. How do you measure love? The price of an evening gown and matching shoes?

Bret felt the beginnings of a vicious headache. It wasn't a hangover. She hadn't done any serious drinking over the weekend, constrained by the presence of her cousins. She didn't want to conjure up the painful memories. That was why she had stopped going to the therapist. Dr. Mervin had tried to force Bret to talk about the past, and she didn't want to do that.

She wanted to get over the past, to move on. To what, she wasn't sure. Anything would be better than what she'd been going through, how she'd been living.

LESLEY

Back at her own apartment in Wadesboro, Lesley felt as though she'd been gone longer than a few days. Her mail consisted of only a few advertising circulars and a couple of fashion catalogs. She flipped through these, then pitched them in the wastebasket. They rarely carried anything smaller than a petite 4. She was finding it harder and harder to find anything that fit without extensive alterations.

As she walked from room to room, Lesley felt pride in her orderly life. Her apartment was neat, her closets tidy, her clothes color coordinated and arranged so that getting dressed and going to work in the morning was never a hassle.

Her apartment was simply furnished, because she liked the uncluttered look. She had a couple of canvas butterfly chairs, and several large pillows that could provide seating when she had more than one guest, which was seldom.

She was due to report back to school on Monday. A quick check of her refrigerator alerted her that she needed to make a trip to the grocery store. Although her shopping list was short and rarely varied, she still wrote it down in her small, neat handwriting so she wouldn't forget anything.

Among a few household supplies she listed one jar of Just Fruit Jelly—no added sugar—a loaf of Slim wheat bread, a carton of nonfat plain yogurt, organic vegetables and fruit and several bottles of water.

Lesley always carried one bottle with her to school and kept it in her desk. She sipped on it when she felt hungry. It was filling and prevented her from eating too much at lunch.

The neighborhood market was not very crowded at this time of day. She moved her cart down the nearly empty aisles gazing at the packed shelves, stopping now and then, tempted, but pushing quickly past. If she ever gave in to the impulse to buy an item, she'd end up throwing it away. Or worse, eating it and then having to get rid of it.

At the produce bin she spotted a shiny green, lightly striped watermelon, sliced to display the deep pink center. She could never manage to eat one in a week, she thought, sighing, and moved on. As she rounded the corner into the bread section, she saw the bakery delivery man stacking fresh loaves of French

bread. Her mouth watered. She halted, mentally rel-
ishing the hard, crisp crust, the soft inside lathered
with thick butter. She picked up one, debated, then
reluctantly replaced it and started to move on when a
teasing male voice said, "Half a loaf is better than
none. Want to split it?"

Lesley turned and saw a young man gazing long-
ingly at the tempting loaves. His blue eyes twinkled
mischievously. Lesley regarded him a moment. He
seemed harmless enough and was very good-looking.
Of medium height and slight build, he wore a V-neck
gray sweater over an open-collared Oxford shirt and
khaki chinos. Then she glanced into his shopping cart.
It contained several boxes of frozen dinners, a half-
gallon of milk, a pint of half and half, a quart of
chocolate ice cream. Nothing to cook. Obviously a
bachelor. On the make?

"No, thanks." She shook her head, gave him a
cool smile and pushed her basket past him. A minute
later, she had second thoughts. Did she know him
from somewhere? Was he possibly one of her kin-
dergartners' young father? She hoped she hadn't appeared rude. But she'd heard that some singles used
grocery shopping as a dating service. She suspected
he'd been making a move on her. And she was certainly not interested in making any such casual con-
nection, no matter how nice a man looked. And that
fellow *had* looked...well, very attractive. However,
she had no time to even think of men. Not while she
was still trying to figure out what to do about her
engagement. Being at Spindrift had given her time to
think about it. Maybe it was the memories the place,
the beach, the cottage evoked that made her seriously
consider she might be making a mistake.

When she went home to Larchmont at Thanksgiving, she would talk to Van, and if she still felt that the engagement might be a mistake, she would find the courage to end it. Lesley wanted to do the right thing—but she had to be sure it was the right thing, not act hastily.

Dear Bret and Lesley,
Just to let you both know how much I enjoyed being with you at Spindrift. I really believe Nonie's purpose in leaving the cottage to us jointly was to bring us together again. I'm going to try doing my part to keep us in touch. What about the idea of a kind of round-robin letter once a month? Wouldn't have to be long, just a paragraph or two telling what's going on in each of our lives. Let me know what you think.
Always,
Anne

Bret to Anne e-mail
Great idea. Like what's happening? New job? New plans? New man?

Dear Anne and Bret,
I have to turn in a teacher's report every month anyway, so a monthly note is no problem. I think it's a good suggestion. I'm all for it.
Love,
Lesley

Chapter Five

October

Anne's first day back at work was a bright sunny one. She loved her job in the Public Relations department of the small liberal arts college.

It didn't matter that she had first come to Glenharbor to escape. Well, if not exactly to escape, at least to get away from a relationship that was going nowhere and never would.

Although Anne had shrugged off Bret's questions about the men in Glenharbor, her cousin's probing had given her something to think about. Over the years she had developed a pattern of falling for unavailable men. Was it the fact that they were unavailable that attracted her? Some such past infatuations came to mind: the swim team coach in high school, the married graduate student in college, the young politician when she was a volunteer worker on his campaign. Did Dale Myers fit into this same category?

Anne remembered the first time she had heard his name. He was the midterm replacement hired after the sudden death of Dr. Pickens, who had been head of the English department for decades.

Almost at once Dale Myers became one of the college's most popular instructors. His classes were always full, students clamoring to sign up for them. Curious about his popularity, Anne asked one of the clerks from the Registrar's Office, "What's with this guy? We always get a handful of requests to audit after the class is full."

Lisa raised her eyebrows, "Have you seen him?"

"I don't think so."

"Oh, if you had, you'd know it." Lisa laughed. "He's…he's got…" She made a kind of grrring sound "Animal magnetism, the kids call it nowadays. When I was in college…I guess *charisma* was the word for it."

"Or else there's a greater interest in poetry than is usually assumed," suggested another of the clerks, and this was greeted by a burst of laughter from all.

After that Anne had heard other things about Dale Myers and had begun to create a mental image of him. An image that intrigued by its very elusiveness.

It was days later when she was at her desk in the library annex that she looked up and saw a young bearded man. He strode straight up to her. In jeans and a flannel shirt he was handsome in a rugged, out-doorsy way; his longish tawny-brown hair was curled around his neck.

"I'm Dale Myers," he announced. "I'm told this

is the place I should leave any curriculum announcements.''

''That's right,'' Anne replied, thinking how weird it was for him to walk into her office when only a short time ago she had been thinking about him. He told her he wanted to leave the topic of his new series of classes so that it could be placed in the campus newsletter. Anne took it and assured him it would be included. She read his cramped, nearly illegible writing on the slip of paper he handed her. ''Women Poets in Nineteenth-Century America. First quarter: Emily Dickinson.''

''Sounds interesting,'' Anne said, hoping to engage him in conversation. But he seemed distracted, in a hurry, and left with only a nod.

Later that day on her way to lunch at the campus cafeteria she saw a poster on the library door announcing a poetry reading in the student lounge. Original poetry by Professor Dale Myers. It seemed an incredible coincidence that twice in one day Dale Myers had crossed her path. Impulsively Anne decided to attend the poetry reading that evening.

She arrived a little late, and the lounge was already crowded. She picked her way through people seated on the floor to a place in the corner but near the podium.

There was an excited murmur among the gathering, then a hush fell when Dale Myers strode to the podium. He had a self-deprecating manner as he introduced himself and talked a little about his poetry. That was when he captured Anne. He was charismatic. Spellbinding. His voice was deep, thrilling, and he read each line as if he enjoyed the taste of it. His gestures were theatrical, the way he brushed back his forelock from his brow, the way he moved.

The last poem he read was obscure and Anne wasn't sure she understood its meaning, but when he looked up from the book he held, he seemed to be looking right at her, speaking the lines directly to her.

"We are all creatures of longing, passion and poetry, waiting as empty vessels for love."

Anne felt a tingle down her spine and across her scalp. She couldn't breathe. That was how she felt, that aching loneliness, reaching out and never finding it. How did he know?

Immediately when he finished, he was surrounded by adoring fans.

Stunned by the emotional impact of his poetry on her, Anne stood patiently in the line that formed to speak to him. As she waited, anything she might say seemed somehow banal. When her turn came all she could do was grip the hand he extended and say, "It was quite wonderful. Thank you."

He frowned and kept her hand in his a little longer, "Are you in one of my classes? I can't place you, but yet I seem to know you...."

Because you know my heart. You reached into my soul, Anne almost blurted out. Instead, she just murmured, "Maybe. I work in the PR office in the library."

"Ah, yes." He smiled that heart-rocking smile. "I spend a great deal of time there. Researching. Thanks very much for coming."

There was a definite flicker of recognition in his eyes. Anne felt her heart thump. Had he actually remembered her? Before she looked away, he gave a smile and he inclined his head in a slight nod. Maybe he *had* remembered their brief encounter.

Anne could feel people behind her getting restless so she moved on. She drove home that night in a kind of soaring wonder. Dale Myers had tapped into something within her that had been locked away for a long time, stirred the possibility that it might be freed.

Anne drove home recalling the foolish fluttering of her heart when Dale Myers seemed to recognize her. Was she following her old adolescent pattern? She banged one fist lightly on the steering wheel. *I'm* not *going down that road again. I promised myself that the last time.*

But in spite of her resolve, the next day Anne made an excuse to go over to the campus bookstore as soon as it opened and buy Dale Myers's three books of poetry. She took them home and devoured them. Although they were difficult sometimes for her to understand, the poet himself came through them.

By the end of the last book, Anne had already fallen a little in love with him.

LESLEY

Lesley loved teaching kindergarten, loved her class of five-year-olds. "Little faces looking up, holding wonder like a cup," as Bret had so aptly quoted. They sparked all sorts of creativity in her. She spent hours preparing her classes and was well rewarded for it. The children were always so enthusiastic. Her work fulfilled her in a way nothing else ever had. She was certainly finding less time to worry about her engagement to Van Madison.

She had been too busy much of the time to worry about anything. Especially about her health. This

came to a screeching halt when something totally unexpected happened.

It was a bright fall day in early October. The
school's autumn carnival was coming up and there
were decorations to make for her classroom and cos-
tumes to design for the children. The classroom wall
clock pointed to four. After tidying up and setting out
the materials for the next day's first project, Lesley
was ready to leave. She gathered up her things, closed
and locked the door of the kindergarten.

As she pushed through the glass door at the entrance of the school building the sun suddenly seemed
to be whirling in the sky, too bright, too fast. She felt
horribly dizzy. She put one arm out to steady herself
on the side of the door, but she couldn't seem to reach
it. She swayed and stumbled against the wall. She
couldn't seem to breathe, a cold sweat washed over
her leaving her shaky and sick. She heard a roaring
in her ears. Her heart thundered. Was she having a
heart attack? Her knees started to buckle.

"Les, what's wrong?" an anxious voice filtered
through her fuzziness. It was her friend Donna, the
fourth-grade teacher. She grabbed Lesley's arm.
"Here lean on me. I'll help you."

"Sorry," Lesley murmured, "I don't know
what—"

"Hush, don't try to talk."

Lesley let Donna hold her arm firmly as she walked
unsteadily to a nearby bench.

"Sit down. Put your head down on your knees,"
Donna directed.

In a few minutes Lesley began to feel better. She
raised her head and things came back into focus. She

looked at Donna. "Thank you, I don't know what happened—"

"You might be catching the flu," Donna suggested. "There's a lot of it going around. Let me drive you home."

"No, thanks, I'm sure I'll be okay," Lesley protested. "It's only a few blocks. You may be right, I'm probably coming down with something."

"You sure I can't take you?" Donna stood, picked up her own books and bag. "It's no trouble."

Lesley shook her head. "No, really I'm fine now. Thanks for your help."

"No problem, I just hope you're okay." Donna still looked concerned.

"I'm fine, really, and thanks."

After Donna walked away, Lesley sat on the bench a few minutes longer, then took a deep breath and stood up. Still a little woozy, she thought the walk home in the fresh air would do her good. Probably she had inhaled too much glue and poster paint in the classroom. Or maybe she *was* coming down with a bug of some kind. One or another of the kids she worked with every day always had a runny nose or a temperature and were sent to school anyway. A teacher's occupational hazard.

But as soon as she got to her apartment she felt worse. Not bothering to do anything but kick off her shoes, she lay down on top of the bed and pulled the quilt up over her shivering shoulders.

The next morning she woke up feeling okay. The next few days passed with no recurrence of the frightening incident. Busy with all the special events in the school's fall program, Lesley kept putting off making a doctor's appointment. Of course, she sometimes felt weak and dizzy. Keeping up with twenty-eight active five-year-olds five days a week took lots of energy. Anyone would feel worn-out. She found she wasn't even looking forward to going home for Thanksgiving.

What she'd really like to do was just hole up in her apartment and sleep for a week.

BRET

Bret woke up to the glare of a harsh sun streaming in through a plate glass window. She heard the muted sounds of a vacuum cleaner being used in the hall outside her hotel room. She turned her head painfully to squint at the face of her travel clock on the bedside table.

A quarter of eleven! She gasped. She'd missed her appointment in downtown Atlanta with the buyer of Glenda's Fashions. Her head dropped back on the pillow. Well, it was too late now. She'd put in a call later, make some excuse about being tied up.

Tied on was more like it. Why had she stayed down in the hotel cocktail lounge so long last night? It hadn't even been that interesting. The salesman from Detroit had been a jerk. Why had she kept on with the conversation? Why had she kept on drinking, even if he was buying? Stupid.

Bret pushed her fingers through her hair. Of course she knew why. She'd kept hoping the Global Airlines crew would check in. Waiting to see if Skip Dalton would be one of them.

Disgusted with herself, she tossed back the covers, letting the silk coverlet slither to the floor. She sat up, swung her legs over the edge of the bed and reached for her robe, struggled into it and onto her feet. *Whoa!*

She felt dizzy. Staggering a little, she went into the bathroom and snapped on the light switch.

A blinding flood of light made her blink. She ducked her head and grabbed the marbleized counter to steady herself. When she raised her head she saw a ravaged face staring relentlessly back at her.

Involuntarily she shuddered. Her hair was wild, her skin had a chalky pallor, her eyes were circled with dark shadows. She groaned and turned away.

She hadn't looked so good last night, either. Not as the hours ticked away and Skip was a no-show. Had she got it wrong? Hadn't he said Atlanta on the fifteenth? Maybe his schedule had been changed, or he had taken another pilot's flight. Something—any-thing—could have happened. She remembered catch-ing a glimpse of herself in the mirror behind the bar and wondering for a minute who that hollow-eyed woman was. It was then that she had left her drink and refused the offer of dinner with the guy from Detroit and tried to walk without weaving through the lobby to the elevator.

She leaned over the basin and splashed cold water onto her face. Her mouth felt like cotton and she swished some water around in it. Then, sliding the shower door open, she stepped inside and turned on the water full force. She felt sore all over. The needle spray bit into her scalp, shoulders, spine. She felt a hundred years old.

How many appointments did she have lined up for today? She'd try to make up for the morning and work straight through until five.

She turned off the shower, then stepped out and wrapped herself in a towel, padded back in to the bedroom, called room service and ordered a large pot of coffee. She got out her appointment book. She needed to check addresses and numbers of the boutiques and stores and other potential customers in the local phone book. She opened the desk drawer to drag out the directory. When she did, she saw the Gideon Bible beside it. She looked at it for a few minutes. Memories washed over her. Her grandmother starting each day at Spindrift reading a verse from Scripture, ending the evening with a favorite Psalm. Bret slammed the drawer shut. Her heart suddenly thudded.

What would Nonie think if she could have seen this granddaughter last night? Or any of a dozen other nights? She would certainly have offered up many prayers for her errant granddaughter. Nonie had believed nothing was more powerful than prayer.

All at once the week alone at Spindrift that Bret had been dreading seemed appealing, an oasis in the dreary desert her life had become. A place to go, away from all this. All what? All the emptiness, all the knocking on doors that would never open, all the pain that wouldn't stop? Bret closed her eyes, pressed fingers against her throbbing temples, felt the wave of nausea.

My own fault. Last night and all the other wasted nights. How stupid to while away preparatory time for today's calls on customers. She knew her sales were slipping. Her supervisor, Linda, had warned her last month. Over the last few months her commissions were less than they had ever been. Ever since Nonie's death, since the weekend at Spindrift with her cousins, things had gone steadily downhill for her.

Skip? She couldn't blame that on Skip. It was her

obsessing about their relationship. He had never promised anything.

That weekend with Anne and Lesley had made her aware of all that was missing in her life, all that she had wanted and somehow lost. Where along the way had she lost herself?

The words came into her head as clearly as if they had been printed along the bottom of a TV screen or in a headline. *Face it. Skip will never commit. Never.*

Bret's hands clenched. She didn't want to face it. She bit her lower lip against a scream that rose in her throat from the depths of her soul. But just then there was a knock at the door. A voice announced, "Room Service." Bret grabbed her robe, slipped it on. Tightening the sash, she went to unlock the door.

Chapter Six

October and November

On Sunday Anne set out for Nada and Tom Winter's house for brunch. She hadn't seen them since her return from North Carolina and so had accepted the invitation happily. It was then that Nada had told her, "I have someone I want you to meet. He's perfectly charming, attractive and someone you would like."

"Uh-oh!" Anne had laughed. Nada was a close friend and Anne adored her but she was also an inveterate matchmaker. She was always trying to fix Anne up with someone. She had had countless small dinner parties, pairing Anne with someone.

"You sound perilously like my mother, Nada."

"Well, your mother is probably right. And so am I."

They had both laughed, then Nada went on, "His name is Elliott Grayson and he's the new manager of the PBS TV station KGHTV."

As she walked the short distance through the woods from her own home to their rustic house, Anne wondered what Nada would think if she knew about her more than casual interest in Dale Myers. Since Tom was a biology professor, Nada knew most of the campus gossip. Dale Myers had swept onto the quiet campus with a flamboyance that was unusual. She was sure Nada could fill her in on what the other faculty members thought of the new English instructor.

Nada met Anne at the door with a hug. Tall, slim, with prematurely gray hair, today Nada was dressed in her usual distinctive style—a denim dress and the silver-and-turquoise Native American jewelry she collected.

"It's still warm so we're eating outside," she told Anne. "Come along and see everyone."

Anne knew most of the small group of people who were gathered out on the deck. After an exchange of greetings Nada led her over and introduced her to Elliott Grayson.

He had a lean, intelligent face, thoughtful eyes and dark hair heavily silvered at the temples. His smile was genuinely friendly.

Surprisingly, Anne liked Elliott Grayson immediately. He was interested in the Public Relations Department of the college, he was intelligent and widely read and he had a great sense of humor. She found she was enjoying herself very much.

"Nada tells me you do most of the copywriting for the college community outreach." He brought out a brochure from the inside pocket of his tweed jacket and held it up. "Then you're probably responsible for this one about Art in the Park?"

"As a matter of fact, I am. Except for the photographs of last year's festival. Those were taken by our staff photographer.''

''A real class act.'' He regarded her with interest. ''I guess I hadn't expected anything so professional.''

''In this small college 'behind the Redwood Curtain'?'' Her tone was half-teasing.

''Not at all. I wasn't going to say that. I'm already in love with this town. I've been looking for someone for the station. I'm thinking of putting out a monthly bulletin, more than a schedule of the programs I hope to be doing. I need someone who knows layout and who can also write copy—'' He stopped abruptly. ''I guess you're not looking for a new job, right?''

''Not really.''

''How long have you been at the college?''

''Nearly three years.''

''And before that?''

''I worked for a small biweekly newspaper.'' As she answered, a picture of Ted, the very married editor, flashed into Anne's mind. Another unavailable man she had spent a great deal of time thinking about who had actually been her reason for eventually leaving the paper.

''Doing what?''

Anne laughed. ''Just about everything.''

''What prompted your move here?'' Elliott halted. ''Sorry. People are always asking me that, and I get tired of answering, yet here I am asking you the same question. What I usually tell them, if I think they're really interested, is that I wanted to find a sense of community, a place where people care about each other—a place where they want to bring up their children. I wanted to find a place where I feel as though I can make a worthwhile contribution.''

"I'm afraid my reasons are not quite that idealistic. But you're right. It's important. As my grandmother used to say, 'Bloom where you're planted.'"

"Exactly. I could have stayed in the city. In fact, I had offers from bigger stations, more money, but—" Elliott shrugged "—I like it here. And I'm beginning to like it more and more." Then he added, "I have joint custody of my daughter, Madeline— Maddie. This will be a nice place for her to come when she visits."

So Elliott had been married, was now divorced. Did that make him eligible? Or with a child, safely un-available?

"How old is Maddie?"

"Eight, going on sixteen." He smiled. "Very bright, maybe a little precocious for her age. That happens to kids sometimes when their parents split up."

Anne saw a muscle in Elliott's jaw tighten. The divorce must have left a residue of bitterness.

"She was only three at the time, so I hope it didn't do too much damage. We tried to keep it civilized for her sake." He paused. "She's quite a little girl." In his expression pride mingled with a little sadness.

"When she comes, I'd like you to meet her, Anne. I'd like her to meet you."

"I'd like that, too," Anne replied.

Just then Nada's voice reached them. "Come on, everyone, brunch is ready."

A wonderful assortment of food was arranged on a huge, round table made from an ancient hay-wagon wheel. Tom's hobby was woodworking and many of the unique furnishings in the Winters' home were his creations.

Anne and Elliott joined the others, who were filling their plates with scrambled eggs, crisp bacon, several kinds of hot breads, cantaloupe crescents and pineapple slices. A samovar of coffee and a pitcher of chilled orange juice sat side by side.

It was a pleasant time and Anne was glad she had come, glad she had met Elliott Grayson. As she left, Nada said, "I'll call you soon."

And Anne knew she would.

The following Saturday Anne looked up from her computer screen and saw Elliott Grayson coming in the door of her office.

"Miss Sherwood, it's much too pretty a day to be working inside," he greeted her. "Besides, if I'm to believe a brochure I got in the mail this week, the Art in the Park show is not to be missed. Am I right, or was that all PR hyperbole?"

"Certainly not!" She smiled and pushed away from her desk. "Every word was true. I'm just finishing up some loose ends. Sometimes it's easier to work when the office is empty. No distractions."

"You are going, then? To the Students' Art in the Park?"

"I was planning to."

"Then come with me." He leaned over the counter that separated Anne's desk from the main room. "I'll take you to lunch."

"Sounds good, thank you. Wait until I turn this off, okay?" She shut down the computer, her screen faded to gray and the words It Is Now Safe to Turn Off Your Computer flashed across it.

She reached in her drawer for her purse and stood up. "I'm ready."

"Where would you like to eat?" he asked as they left the library and walked out into the sunshine.

"We could get a taco or something at one of the concession booths."

Elliott seemed doubtful. "I had something else in mind."

"They have really good food at these affairs. I think you should try some."

"Okay. When in Rome..." He grinned. "I'll take your word for it." He took her arm. "My car's over there."

"We can walk," she told him. "The exhibits start at the edge of the campus only a few blocks from here. And as you pointed out, it is a lovely day."

They started down the path that wound down the hill leading to the quadrangle where the fair booths were set up.

"What project are you working on now?" he asked.

"Oh, a brochure on a combined evening performance of the music and drama departments."

"I hope I'm on the mailing list."

"Of course. We'd love some TV coverage, maybe even some live interviews?"

"Be sure to give me the dates. We could schedule some promo beforehand, three-minute spots starting two weeks ahead?"

"That would be wonderful."

"Good business. I told you I wanted to make KGHTV a real part of the community. This is the kind of thing that lets the powers-that-be and potential advertisers know that we're here for the long haul."

Elliott did most of the talking until they got into the stretch of sidewalk with the first exhibit. Then they concentrated on the colorful posters, unique sand sculpture and lovely paintings of local scenes displayed in the booths that filled the quadrangle.

"All this artistic expression is making me very hungry," Elliott said at last. "Shall we get something to eat then find a place to sit?"

When they had stocked up plastic trays with mammoth submarine sandwiches, mounds of coleslaw and large cartons of icy cola, they wandered a little apart from the parade of art viewers and vendors, found a bench overlooking the duck pond and sat down.

"You were right," Elliott said between bites. "This is really good."

"Would I lie?" Anne teased.

They both laughed.

"Dessert?" Elliott asked. "We passed a booth with some fantastic cakes, pies and mysterious things with whipped cream pyramids topped with strawberries. Are you game?"

"Game, but not able." Anne shook her head. "I couldn't eat another bite. At least, not now."

"We'll get something later then, when we've done the rest of the show. This is fun. I didn't know if it would be, but it is."

"Why did you come, if you weren't sure?"

"Your persuasive copy." He grinned. "And the chance of seeing you again."

Anne felt her face warm. Trying to seem nonchalant, she wiped her hands on the paper napkin and brushed at her skirt.

"It's hard when you're the boss to call in sick or just take the day off. I'll be taking a long weekend when Maddie comes to spend Thanksgiving with me. This year it's my turn. My ex-wife and I try to be fair, share holidays.'' He sighed. ''We have what's called 'an amicable divorce.'''

Anne didn't comment, although she was curious. Who had wanted the divorce...and why? Elliott seemed everything any woman would want in a husband. But then, only the two people in any relationship knew what really went on within it.

''I'm a little at a loss as to how to keep her occupied while she's with me. When I lived in the Bay Area there were so many places to take her—the zoo at Golden Gate Park, the Exploratorium. Here, I'm not sure. Children change so quickly, especially when you only see them months apart. And here I don't know any other parents of children her age with whom I could arrange things for her to do.''

Elliott looked anxious. Suddenly Anne saw a new side of the man: the devoted father instead of the sophisticated businessman.

''There's a children's theater,'' Anne said thoughtfully. ''I'd have to double check, but I believe they have an upcoming production of *Charlotte's Web*. Would you like me to find out?''

''That would be great, Anne. Thank you.''

Elliott looked so grateful Anne was touched.

''Maybe if you can get tickets we could all go,'' he suggested.

Anne just smiled. She did not want to commit herself to any plans with Elliott and his daughter. Why not? she asked herself, but refused to answer her own question.

''I'll let you know.'' She stood, crumpled up what was left of her lunch and pushed it into one of the trash bins nearby. ''Shall we go take a look at the other booths?''

They went back to the center of the plaza, which had been turned into an outdoor gallery. A small acrylic seascape caught Anne's attention. It was quite good. It reminded her of the jetty at the end of the curve of the beach a short distance from Spindrift.

Elliott turned back to her and asked, "Do you like that?"

"Yes, it makes me think of the beach near my grandmother's cottage where I used to go when I was a little girl."

Elliott had taken out his wallet, saying to one of the artists, "I'd like to buy this painting."

"It's fifty dollars," she said tentatively. Evidently not too many sales had been made, and she was unsure that this one would go through.

"Well worth it," he told her. "I'll take it." He pulled out three bills and handed it to the happy student artist. She unhooked the painting from the peg on which it had been hung and slipped it into a plastic bag. Elliott tucked it under his arm as they walked on.

It wasn't until after he walked Anne back to the library and handed the seascape to her that she realized he had bought it for her.

"Oh, but you shouldn't have. It's too expensive a gift...."

"Don't fuss, Anne. The money goes to a good cause. The art students told me they're trying to earn enough for a trip to San Francisco to see the Van Gogh exhibit that's coming there. Besides, I wanted you to have it." He paused, smiling. "If you could have seen your face when you were looking at it, you'd understand why."

"That's awfully kind, thank you. She slipped the

painting out of the plastic wrapping and looked at it again. "This looks like the view from the window in my grandmother's cottage, Spindrift. She died at the end of the summer and left it to me and my two cousins."

"Then I'm glad that I followed my impulse. I'm not usually impulsive—often to my own regret. I've been criticized for not being spontaneous. So you see, giving this to you is helping me mend my ways."

Back at her desk Anne realized Elliott Grayson was everything Nada had said—charming, intelligent, interesting. He had asked if he could call her, take her out to dinner some time. She had said yes. It might be pleasant to get to know him better, then the thought of Dale interjected itself and she found herself thinking of him instead.

It was not yet dark and a lingering sunset tinted the tops of the trees. As Anne walked home through the woodland path, she was deeply thoughtful. Coming out from the woods into her neighborhood, she caught the smell of wood smoke. Fires were being lit in the fireplaces of the houses that marched up the hillside, lamps were being turned on, dinner was being cooked, husbands were coming home…and she was returning to an empty house.

In her heart Anne knew she was ready for the great love she had always dreamed of having someday. Was that day now?

Nada called her the next day. "I saw you and Elliott at the fair yesterday. You two certainly looked as though you were having a marvelous time together."

"We were. He's a very nice man."

"Oh, come on, Anne. In my opinion, Elliott Grayson is one of the most attractive men I've seen in this town in a long time. It was apparent Sunday that he found you attractive as well. In fact, found you fascinating."

"As usual, you exaggerate, Nada."

"Not at all. You just don't give yourself enough credit. You're a beautiful young woman and obviously Elliott thinks so, too. Anyone would have to be blind not to see that he was attracted to you."

"Please, Nada, don't jump to any conclusions. And for heaven's sake, don't mention it to Tom."

"Don't worry, I wouldn't."

"Good," Anne said firmly.

"I know I must come off sometimes as a busybody, Anne. But I am old enough to be your mother and I want you to be happy. I see someone like Elliott come into your life and I don't want you to miss the boat. I pray all the time that you'll start believing in yourself."

"Pray, Nada?"

"Of course. Don't you, Anne? To quote Tennyson, 'More things are wrought by prayer than this world dreams of.' I believe that."

Anne was taken aback. Nada was such an assured, self-confident woman Anne was astonished that she would speak so openly about prayer.

"I didn't know you were religious, Nada."

"Just a sinner saved by grace, Anne."

To Anne, Nada and Tom had always seemed the perfect couple, mutually respectful, affectionate. They seemed to like each other, like being together.

Now she wondered if there was another element in their relationship, a spiritual one, which perhaps gave it a special quality. She knew they attended the small church where Tom was a lay reader and Nada led the Christmas choir.

Still, what Nada suggested surprised her. It reminded her of Nonie, who had also believed in prayer. Anne remembered her grandmother and Bernessa praying together in the kitchen at Spindrift.

''Ask and you shall receive, seek and you shall find, knock and it shall be opened to you.'' The memory of those words was as fresh and clear to Anne as when she had first heard them.

Pray? There were so many things she needed, wanted, longed for. But was it right to pray for them? To pray for an enduring love you could trust? It sounded too easy to Anne, too simple, to pray for the kind of love she was seeking.

The following weekend the last college social event for the fall was being held at the president's house, which was actually a mansion built by a nineteenth-century lumber baron whose descendents had endowed most of the college property. Anne's tiny house, once an employee's home was part of the original estate.

It was a must-do event for anyone connected with the college and Anne was obliged to go.

She dressed in a winter-white dress, fixed her hair in a simple pulled-back style and tied it with a black velvet ribbon. What a fuss about nothing, she thought as she caught her reflection in the mirror. After growing up in Brenda's shadow, she never wanted to obsess about her looks. Taking along an antique clutch bag, she left the cottage and headed over the clipped green lawn to the reception. She walked around to the front of the house and went up the steps of the huge, wraparound porch. The front door with its oval stained-glass window stood open and she went inside.

The party was in full swing. Anne paused for a minute on the threshold then headed for the dining room where a beautifully appointed refreshment table had been set up.

She glanced around and saw a few people she knew, but they all seemed to be engaged in conversation. She recognized some students serving as waitresses and waiters, though they looked strangely unfamiliar in their black-and-white uniforms instead of their usual tattered jeans and T-shirts.

She had just had the student who was bartending fill her glass with orange juice when she turned and saw Dale Myers enter. Her heart lodged in her throat. He looked great, wearing a corduroy jacket, a shirt and tie. She had never seen him in other than his casual attire. He stood there for a full minute glancing around, then he seemed to see her and start toward her. Anne's blood turned to ice water. But someone grabbed Dale's arm and he was pulled into a circle of people. Then a tall man stepped into her line of vision and she lost sight of Dale.

Her next thought was how soon could she pay her respects to her hosts, President and Mrs. Harding, and get out of there. She felt foolish to be so aware of Dale's presence.

"Hello there." She heard his voice behind her and whirled around. "I'm glad you're here. Ever since the night of my poetry reading, I've been trying to place you. Now, today, here, I remember you, although I don't think I know your name."

"Anne. Anne Sherwood," she said breathlessly. Incredibly, he remembered her.

"Anne. Almost as old-fashioned a name as Emily." He smiled. "You see, you remind me of Emily Dickinson."

Anne was startled. She thought she was mistaken that he had even noticed her that evening. "I did?"

"Yes. The Belle of Amherst." He smiled, "With your hair pulled back, the cameo, the high-necked white dress. Dickinson made a point of always wearing white. There's only one picture of her, you know, a daguerreotype, and you looked a great deal like her."

"It wasn't intentional," Anne said, remembering she had worn her white dress, Nonie's cameo pin. "But I do love her poems."

They began to talk—or rather Dale talked and Anne listened.

He told her he had graduated from one of the prestigious Eastern colleges, backpacked all over Europe for a year, gone back to one of the New England universities to get his master's degree and spent a year teaching in England until he was recruited by Glenharbor.

"Certainly a far cry from your previous experience," Anne commented.

"I needed a change. I wanted somewhere tranquil, out of the mainstream, a place to write...." He pushed back his chair, stood up. "What a terrific listener you are, Anne."

Anne drew in a breath. Again Dale's gaze lingered on her, and she felt her face flush.

"Could we go somewhere and talk some more?" he said abruptly.

"Yes, I'd like that." She could hardly believe what was happening.

"Sam's Place?" Dale mentioned a campus coffee shop styled like a fifties diner.

"Fine."

"My car?"

"I have my own."

"Okay, I'll meet you there in fifteen minutes," Dale said, then spun around. She saw him shake hands with President Harding, exchange a few words with Mrs. Harding, then go out the door.

She followed in a daze.

Twenty minutes later she was sitting opposite Dale in the glare of the brightly lit student hangout talking about poetry.

"The more you study Dickinson's work and delve into her life, the more you will find she was a deeply passionate woman, though secretive," Dale was saying. "Emily will only open up to you as you extend yourself and commit to her. Not unlike a romance. When you're in love, you give it your all, without holding back…. In other words, you have to fall in love with Emily Dickinson to really know and understand her poetry."

His voice was like spun silk, and in no time Anne was trapped in the web of his words. The night was pure magic, like a dream come true. So much so that driving home, she missed two boulevard stops and almost ran a red light.

Her fog continued as the next morning, Saturday, she slept heavily and woke up late. When she went into the kitchen to make coffee, the message light on her phone was blinking steadily. She prepared the coffee, then, yawning, pushed the Play button and listened.

"Hi, Dale Myers here. Been thinking about you. Lots. Wondering if we could get together sometime." Pause. "Sorry to have missed you. I'll try again. Hope to see you soon."

Anne stared at the coffee dripping through into the glass pot, mesmerized. She was excited but scared, too. Scared she might blow it. Again. In the past whenever men were attracted to her, something had always happened; her insecurity had made the attraction short-lived. It was usually someone she had done a great deal of dreaming about, who was unavailable for some reason. If reality surfaced, she backed off. Being attracted from afar was safer.

She had daydreamed about Dale Myers so much, imagined conversations with him about life, love, poetry, thoughts and feelings...dreamed of herself being witty, subtle and interesting, saying the right things. But delivering all that in person?

She pressed the rewind button, once more listening to his whole message. "Sorry to have missed you. I'll try again. Hope to see you soon."

Anne poured herself a cup of coffee, slid onto one of the high kitchen stools and, leaning on the counter, slowly sipped her coffee. It was good and strong and cleared her sleep-fuzzy brain. What was Dale looking for, what did he expect? Was this time going to work for her?

Or was she letting herself in for another heartbreak?

True to his word, Dale called back with an invitation to dinner. "I want to take you to this great little

Italian place, Ronzoni's. The best authentic food and wine I've had since I was in Venice last summer.''

"I'd love to," Anne said, hoping her voice didn't betray how thrilled she was.

Ronzoni's was like a set in one of those old romantic movies Anne loved to watch on late-night TV. Small, dark, intimate with round tables for two covered with red checkered cloths. In the center of each was a multi-colored candle dripping ribbons of rainbow-colored wax down the sides of a wine bottle. The meal was as delicious as Dale promised. He did most of the talking and Anne was a rapt audience. He had led an adventurous life and she found it fascinating.

He looked at Anne, his eyes soft and dark in the glow from the candlelight. "I'm so comfortable being with you, Anne. It's so rare to find someone who genuinely appreciates what I'm doing, understands who I am, what I'm all about as a poet." He reached across the table and lightly took her hand. "I hope you don't think I'm just using you."

Use me! Anne wanted to say. "I'm flattered you feel you can talk to me like this, Dale."

That night when Dale brought her home, he kissed her lightly and said, "Great being with you, Anne. You know you're really special."

She stood on the porch before going inside and watched him run down the steps and jump into his small English sportscar and drive away. Tonight had been like a dream come true. Just a few weeks ago to imagine Dale Myers would find her interesting enough to spend time with would have seemed impossible.

Just as impossible was the notion that two men would find her appealing.

Elliott Grayson, too, called several times wanting to take her out to dinner or to a movie. But Anne turned him down.

"I wouldn't be good company, Elliott, I'd probably nod off during dinner. I'm working so hard on the Christmas extravaganza with the music department that I've had to narrow my social life."

He accepted her excuses with good humor. "Well, may I be first in line when it's over?"

Anne couldn't think that far ahead. She found herself living for the moment. Waking each day and looking forward to the notes in her mailbox at the college. Notes from Dale.

They were always unsigned but usually had a line of poetry quoted or rephrased. She recognized Dale's scrawled handwriting, found the notes amusing and definitely romantic. Then Dale began to phone her late at night. The first time he startled her out of a sound sleep.

"Did I wake you? I'm sorry. I've been grading papers all evening and the time just got away from me. I'll hang up and you can go back to sleep."

"No, no, it's okay. Really. I'm happy to hear from you."

After that the calls were frequent, and came at all hours, but Anne welcomed them as the proof that she was becoming important to Dale. Sometimes he read her parts of poetry he said he'd been working on, and she listened, thrilled, flattered that he had chosen her as his audience.

Dale took to dropping by Anne's after his evening classes. In the mornings he jogged for exercise, and gradually her house became his stopping place. She always had the coffeemaker filled and ready to snap on at a moment's notice and kept a supply of the biscotti and fudge brownies he loved.

She relished rainy afternoons when they sat in her funky little kitchen, talking. She always hated having their conversations come to an abrupt end when he suddenly checked his watch and jumped up from his chair.

"Gotta go. Have my poetry group meeting tonight."

Anne would often offer to fix him something to eat before he left. But he was usually halfway out the door, shrugging into his jacket or zipping up his windbreaker. Then he would be off. She knew he led a separate poetry group that met at different members' houses. She wondered who was in the poetry group and longed for Dale to invite her to join them. But he never did and she was too shy to ask.

Elliott Grayson continued to call and suggested going out. But Anne always had some excuse. At another time she might have been interested, but preoccupied as she was with Dale Myers, Anne was reluctant to accept. She wanted to leave her time open in case Dale called. He was notoriously negligent about making plans, waiting until the last minute to call, and often breaking the plans he did make.

Still, he held an irresistible attraction for Anne. For all his confident air Dale seemed emotionally needy. He often spoke of the isolation of the artistic soul of a poet—the lack of acceptance, understanding, appreciation he felt among his fellow faculty members.

"Engineering, biology and sociology, they're okay, they make you a member of the club." His voice held a tinge of bitterness. "But mention Coleridge or Hopkins, or Dickinson for that matter, and you get a blank stare.'' He switched topics. "By the way, did you know the spring play is going to be *The Belle of Amherst*? Or rather, a new version of Emily's story—no rights to pay that way? Actually I've been asked if I'd be interested in writing the script and selecting some of Emily's poems to incorporate into the play. And they want me to be the advisor on the project. In fact, they're setting up a meeting for me with the director.''

One night Dale called after midnight.

"May I come over? I know it's late, but I'm feeling lonely. I'd like very much to be with you.''

Of course it was all right with Anne. She jumped out of bed, stripped off her flannel pjs, put on her new royal-blue turtleneck sweater and matching pants. She made a clean sweep of her little parlor, picking up books and discarding newspapers, plumping up pillows, turning on lamps. She threw stacked kindling under two logs and got a fire started in the fireplace. By the time Dale arrived, it was snapping cheerfully, casting a warm glow and making the small room invitingly cozy.

Dale sighed and settled down on the sofa. "Ah, this is wonderful. Anne, you have a talent for creating an atmosphere. Come here.'' He drew her down and pulled her close.

That kiss was something she had hoped would happen but had not been sure ever would. It was tender and lingering. Dale whispered, "I think I'm falling in love with you.''

Anne had never imagined hearing those words from a man she idealized. It had seemed like a dream she had of the perfect romance, an enduring love as beautiful as a poem set to music.

A few days later Dale brought a folder containing a batch of his poetry. He wanted her to read it. Wanted to know if she liked it.

"Of course I will, Dale."

"Well, I'm getting ready to submit them to some prestigious literary magazines. You know the rule for college professors: Publish or perish. The fact is, I just don't have the time to get these properly typed and into manuscript shape and submit them—"

"I'd be happy to do that for you, if you trust me," Anne offered.

"Would you, Anne? It would be enormously helpful."

Dale's handwriting was almost illegible, his punctuation unique and highly original. Anne was a little nervous that she would somehow do them wrong. As it turned out, after she had done the first draft, he made corrections all over it and it had to be typed again. It was tedious work and meant putting in hours at her computer long after regular office hours. But she was thrilled that Dale had given her this special assignment. His own private poetry that no one else had yet seen.

The annual winter rains began early but Anne could have cared less. She was seeing Dale twice a week after his class and any other time he nonchalantly dropped in at her little hillside house. It had become a refuge, he told her, from the life of the college, which he disdained. She was also busy typing up a long narrative poem he had written recently. It took all her free time.

Nada was one of the first to notice Anne's preoccupation. One day when she called to make a lunch date and met Anne's refusal, she demanded, "What in the world are you doing every weekend? You don't seem to have time for anything or anybody anymore."

"I'm helping Dale Myers with a project of his."

"Well, at least you'll take Thanksgiving weekend off, won't you? Of course you will—no excuses. Tom and I are expecting you for Thanksgiving dinner."

Anne reluctantly agreed. She wished she could ask Nada to include Dale in her invitation, but that would start the gossip mill turning.

As it turned out, Dale had plans of his own for the long holiday weekend. He was going out of town with friends, he told her.

The college was closed for Thanksgiving week. The Wednesday before the holiday Anne went to the florist's shop at the mall to pick out a centerpiece to bring as a hostess gift.

Just as she was about to go in the door of the shop, she heard her name called and turned to see Elliott Grayson holding a little girl by the hand.

Of course, Maddie! After sending him a note listing some local activities for children, Anne had been so busy compiling and typing Dale's manuscript, she had almost forgotten about Maddie's visit.

She felt a little guilty that she had not returned any of the recent messages Elliott had left on her answering machine. She halted and waited until he and his little girl caught up with her.

"What a happy coincidence." Elliott greeted her with a wide smile. "Anne, I'd like you to meet my daughter, Maddie." Then turned to the child. "Honey, this is the lady I told you about, the one who suggested we go to the play about Wilbur." He smiled at Anne. "It couldn't have been a better choice. As luck would have it, Maddie's read *Charlotte's Web* and loved the story."

"I'm glad." Anne included the little girl in her smile. Maddie was thin, her dark hair was cut in bangs that fell unevenly to the top of her round glasses, which kept slipping down on her small nose. Behind the lenses were large brown eyes that were now regarding Anne steadily.

Anne held out her hand. "Hello, Maddie. I'm happy to meet you. I know your dad is glad you're here."

Maddie smiled shyly but did not say anything. Anne saw that her two front teeth were missing and new ones were just peeping through the gums.

She was probably just shy, Anne decided, and tried again with a compliment. "What a pretty outfit you're wearing."

"My mother brought it back for me from Paris," Maddie replied.

Anne's glance moved to Elliott for an explanation of this surprising statement.

"Valerie is a flight attendant for Worldwide Airlines. She makes regular transatlantic trips."

"Oh, well, how nice for Maddie," Anne remarked, not knowing where to go with this bit of information about Elliott's ex-wife.

She stood there uncertainly for a minute. "Well, have a good day. Nice meeting you, Maddie." She took a few steps toward the entrance to the florist's shop.

"Anne, could we repay you for recommending the play by treating you to a banana split at Heavenly

Delights?'' Elliott gestured to the soda fountain nearby. ''That's where we're headed.''

''Sorry, I have a long list of errands. Thanks anyway.''

Elliott tried another tack. ''They might have frozen yogurt.''

She had once mentioned to him she was a frozen-yogurt addict. Anne laughed. ''You have a remarkable memory. But still I'll have to pass.''

''Maddie will be here through next week—maybe the three of us could have lunch or dinner or something,'' he suggested hopefully.

Anne hesitated. Maybe Dale would get back into town early as he had hinted. She wanted to be free if he did. If she committed to a possible date with Elliott it would complicate things. So she didn't answer, just smiled again at Maddie and said, ''It was so nice meeting you. I hope you have a wonderful visit with your daddy.''

Then Anne said goodbye and left them. Elliott had looked genuinely disappointed, and Anne felt a pang of regret that she had not taken him up on his invitation. She could at least have gone with them to the ice cream parlor.

She was distracted while deciding about a flower arrangement to take to Nada. She couldn't stop thinking about Elliott and his little girl. She wondered what they would do on Thanksgiving. Did he have friends who might invite them to dinner? Would he cook a turkey himself? Or would the two of them go to a restaurant? That mental picture seemed rather forlorn, and Anne wished she didn't have plans herself so she could have invited them to her house. One thing

Brenda had succeeded in teaching her was how to cook.

Little Maddie was especially on her mind as Anne did her other errands. Even though she had not inherited her father's good looks or in all probability those of her glamorous, ocean-hopping mother, there was something very appealing about the little girl.

Maybe Maddie would grow up into her own individual beauty, not intimidated by a beautiful mother as Anne herself had been. Surely the little girl was getting a great deal of care and attention from her father. But Anne hoped she was receiving tender, loving care from someone at home. Maybe a grandmother like Anne had had in Nonie?

If it hadn't been for Nonie's constant reassurance emphasizing the importance of inner beauty, Anne could have been completely overshadowed by *her* glamorous mother.

Thoughts of Maddie and Elliott persisted all through the holiday weekend. Somehow she resisted the temptation to call him and suggest doing something with them.

Anne to cousins I'm spending the holiday with my friends Tom and Nada Winter. Hope you both have a lovely Thanksgiving.

Lesley to cousins I'm going home to Larchmont to my parents for Thanksgiving.

No word from Bret.

Chapter Seven

November

From the expressway Lesley took the off ramp to Larchmont, then eased her foot off the accelerator and slowed to a leisurely fifty-five. She was in no hurry to get home to meet the barrage of questions from her mother about wedding plans—a subject she didn't want to talk about or even think about.

But driving along the winding road between hills brilliant with autumn color at this season of the year brought back memories just as being at Spindrift had. Memories of things she hadn't thought of for years, hadn't allowed herself to think about. The cottage and walking the beach, past the boarded-up skating rink, the lifeguard station—especially the lifeguard station. Craig. The tanned, dark-eyed, curly-haired boy with whom she'd fallen hopelessly in love. Now, driving this road at this particular time of year brought back the memory of another Thanksgiving, the disastrous one when Craig had come to Larchmont.

She had read somewhere that a woman never forgets her first love or her first heartbreak. Craig had been both.

But how long did it go on hurting? Shouldn't Van have replaced Craig. Erased him? The trouble was, he hadn't.

Craig was a talented artist, working two jobs that summer at Sea Watch Cove. A lifeguard during the day, a waiter three nights a week at the Beachcomber Restaurant. He was saving money for his tuition to Pratt Institute in New York. It had been almost instant attraction between them. After they met, they spent as much time together as they could. On his one day off a week they would take a picnic to their favorite place, the old stone jetty. Craig would bring his sketchbook, colored pens and draw. He drew everything, sailboats on the horizon, rocks, surf and sometimes Lesley. She still had one of the sketches he'd done of her, put away somewhere, maybe in a box in her bedroom closet at home in Larchmont, along with other memorabilia of her life. Barbie dolls, scrapbooks of movie stars, her high school yearbook...

At the end of the summer Craig kissed her goodbye and whispered, "I love you." Words she had waited all summer to hear. Then they parted, he to New York, Lesley to college. At Thanksgiving he had hitchhiked partway, ridden the Greyhound bus the rest of the way to Larchmont.

She should have known better than to expect her parents to accept Craig, to see and appreciate him as she did. He didn't fit the Larchmont mold. In jeans and a sweater he seemed out of place. He was ill at ease in the Sherwood home with its polished furniture, Sèvres china, uniformed maid.

Lesley was in a frenzy of anxiety throughout his visit. Nervous about what impression he was making on her parents, she had not been herself. Certainly not the carefree girl Craig knew from the summer. Even before he left to go back to New York, Lesley had the feeling the weekend had been a disastrous mistake. She regretted the awkward position in which she had put Craig by inviting him to her home. Even though he called her from a pay phone at the bus station and told her he loved her, she felt she had lost him.

After that weekend, the letters and the phone calls gradually lessened, and eventually stopped. When she tried phoning Craig, Lesley was told his number had been disconnected. Disconnected. That was how she felt now. Disconnected from all that was going on in her life.

Her gaze fell onto her left hand, where the dark-blue sapphire and surrounding tiny diamonds glittered in the sun. She drew in her breath. I shouldn't have accepted it. Not when I'm so unsure it's the right thing.

Lesley braked suddenly. She had been so distracted she had passed the road she should have taken. She made a U-turn and headed back to make a right. Sycamore Drive was a tree-lined street flanked on both sides by large houses set back on velvety lawns. It was one of the most prestigious residential sections of Larchmont. Where the old money lived and where the nouveaux riches wanted to.

To her surprise when she pulled to a stop in front of their house, both her parents were outside. Her mother, in her sweater set and pleated plaid skirt, her father in a cashmere crewneck sweater over his shirt. They both waved and smiled.

After being affectionately greeted and hugged, Lesley got a long critical look from her mother. "You look exhausted, dear. You work much too hard."

Lesley murmured something she hoped was soothing and turned to get her suitcase out of the trunk of her car.

"By the way, Terry phoned." Terry had been Lesley's best friend since childhood. She was getting married in December, and of course Lesley was in the wedding.

"Oh, good. I wasn't sure she'd be home."

"Seems she's taken a leave of absence from that dreadful job in New York until after her wedding. I know her mother's relieved. She's worried sick about her living in the inner city."

Lesley didn't comment other than to say, "I'll call her right away." She knew Terry's mother did not understand that Terry felt she had a calling to teach underprivileged students.

As she walked into her bedroom, Lesley had a sense of déjà vu. She surveyed the gray French Provincial furniture, the canopy bed with its stenciled nosegays of flowers and flowing blue ribbons. And her row of Madame Alexander dolls along the top shelf of her bookcase.

The white phone was on her bedside table right where it had always been. She dialed the number she'd known by heart since fifth grade.

Later, when her mother stopped by her room, Lesley told her, "Terry wants me to have lunch with her tomorrow. She's made reservations at Gwendolyn's."

"That's lovely, dear. I know you two have a great deal to talk about. You also have an appointment for a fitting at Vinnie's for your bridesmaid's dress."

Terry was already at a table in the corner. She broke into a wide smile and waved and motioned Lesley over.

As Lesley approached, Terry jumped up and gave her a hug.

"It's so great to see you, Les!" she said as they sat down. "There's going to be a bridesmaids bash at the club Saturday. Mom insisted on it." Terry wrinkled her nose in her characteristic sign of resignation. "And I went along with it. I don't want any more grief about this wedding." She grimaced as if there were more to tell on that score at some other time. "Both Mom and Ben's mother are fussing about how hard the Faith and Grace Tabernacle is going to be to decorate for the wedding. It's a geodesic dome, you know, built to accommodate the growing congregation—no nave, no center aisle." She shrugged. "But enough about all that, I've been so anxious to see you. There's so much to tell."

There always was when the two were together no matter how long they had been apart. They'd met in kindergarten, gone all through elementary and high school, been in Girl Scouts together and later were roommates at college. However, before they could start catching up a waitress appeared, dressed like a Victorian parlor maid in a black dress, crisply starched eyelet-trimmed apron and cap. They placed their orders and she went away.

"You look so happy," Lesley remarked almost wistfully, looking at Terry.

"Oh, I am, Les." Terry leaned forward, eyes sparkling.

There was definitely something different about her. It was more than the happy glow of a bride-to-be. Now Terry looked absolutely radiant.

Terry reached across the table and squeezed Les's hand. "The most wonderful thing of all is Ben has accepted the Lord." She rushed on. "Ben was always great, but when we decided to get married, there was so much discussion about where and who would marry us. My mother and *his* mother went on endlessly. It really got...well, too much. I almost felt like calling it off and eloping." She giggled. "Then Ben just stepped in—I was so proud of him—and he said, 'It's Terry's choice, *our* wedding.'" Terry paused because the waitress returned with their plates. When she left again, Terry continued. "I was pretty upset and went to talk to my pastor. You know ever since I made a commitment to Christ at youth camp, I've been going to Faith and Grace. Ben went with me and—Pastor was wonderful. He said how we felt about each other and what kind of a life we wanted to have together was the most important thing. He asked Ben point-blank if he was prepared to take the leadership role in our Christian marriage. When he found out Ben had never accepted Christ as his personal savior, he just asked him, 'Do you want to do that now?'" Terry gave a delighted laugh. "And Ben did. So now it's all settled and everyone is happy. Well, just about everybody."

Much as she rejoiced in her friend's happiness, Lesley felt a tiny stab of envy. She wished she felt that same assurance about her own engagement and eventual marriage.

Their conversation soon turned to catch-up, sharing what they knew about mutual Larchmont friends.

The hour went by quickly. Terry expressed regret that she couldn't linger over coffee as she would like.

"I promised Mom I'd meet her at the mall. We have to pick out decorations for the tables at the reception."

"Anyway, I have a final fitting at Vinnie's on my gown," Lesley told her.

From the restaurant Lesley drove to Vinnie Markham's house. She was the town's finest and most sought after seamstress. Terry's gown and the gowns for the bridal party were all being made by Vinnie.

Vinnie had known Lesley and her girlfriends from the time they were youngsters, made their dresses when they had been flower girls in cousins' or older sisters' weddings.

That was why Lesley was surprised when Vinnie opened the door and didn't seem to recognize her. Vinnie stood there for a second or two, a puzzled expression on her pleasant face.

"Vinnie, it's me, Lesley Sherwood. I've come for my fitting for Terry's bridal party."

"Oh, dear heaven, Les, for a minute I didn't know who you were. Come in, come in, I apologize. I've got your dress basted, but we best see if I've got the measurements right."

But in her sewing room when Lesley took off her suit jacket and skirt and stood in her slip, Vinnie gave her a strange look . Ready to drop the rosy tulle and taffeta dress over her head, Vinnie drew in her breath. "Looks to me like you've fallen off quite a bit." As the dress slithered down Lesley's body, Vinnie clutched the excess material, gathering it in at the waist. "Goodness, I didn't know I could be that far off."

Lesley looked at herself in the full-length mirror and was startled. The design of the portrait neckline showed how her shoulder bones jutted and the sinews in her neck stood out. The effect wasn't pretty at all. It was ugly.

Vinnie mumbled under her breath, grabbing bunches of material, pinning them.

The fitting turned out not to be a happy occasion. Foreseeing a major alteration of a dress she thought nearly finished, Vinnie was cross. She complained about all the work involved with the five other girls' gowns and the deadline drawing near.

"I just hope none of 'em goes on some stupid crash diet, too," she grumbled as she helped Lesley out of the pinned-up dress.

Lesley dressed hurriedly and said goodbye.

Driving home, Les felt depressed. Not only about the extra work she was causing Vinnie but the reason.

Was she really as emaciated as she seemed to look in the mirror? She'd have to weigh herself when she got home.

The Friday after Thanksgiving her mother asked Lesley, "Would you take Toto out for her walk, please, dear?"

Their small Tibetan terrier, Toto, named for Dorothy's little dog in Lesley's favorite childhood movie, *The Wizard of Oz,* was nearly nine—old for a dog— and a little snappish.

"Sure, Mom."

Lesley put on the dog's leash. Her own mood

needed lifting, and maybe a brisk walk would do her good as well.

They walked along streets beginning to be papered with fallen leaves. Toto trotted along happily and Lesley kept up her pace. As they turned into an older section of town, Lesley saw the small church, Saint Mary's. It was built of old brick, mellowed with age and covered with Virginia creeper vines now turning crimson at the edges of its leaves. As they came to it she saw into the garden in back. A wooden plaque on the wrought-iron gate read, Garden of Prayer—Come in to Rest, Reflect and Refresh.

She must have passed this church hundreds of times when she was a little girl on her way to the Grove Hill playground. The Randall Sherwoods attended the big gray stone church downtown, and Lesley had never been to Saint Mary's.

She stood there gazing at it, longing to go inside. Dare she enter the garden? As she stood there trying to decide, she saw a woman in the garden trimming the rosebushes with large shears.

Dressed in a brown cotton gardening smock, her graying brown hair pulled up in a careless knot, she moved with a kind of unhurried grace, completely focussed on what she was doing.

The woman had such an aura of serenity about her Lesley was hesitant to interrupt.

As Lesley turned to leave the woman in the garden looked up and waved one gloved hand.

Automatically, Lesley waved back then walked on. She felt strangely drawn to the woman. Her smile, in a Katharine Hepburn kind of high-cheekboned face, was lovely. The brim of her straw hat had shadowed her eyes, but somehow Lesley knew they would be kind and also understanding. There would be wisdom in them.

The scene she had observed stayed with her for the rest of her walk. The woman had been peacefully centered in the present moment.

As if in the presence of God.

Lesley was startled. Where on earth had that thought come from? The answer was swift. Not from earth. "The peace that passeth understanding." That was from Scripture, Lesley knew even though she had not read her Bible recently.

If only she could find a peace like that.

BRET

It was the week before Thanksgiving, the heaviest travel holiday of the year, and the airport terminal bustled with the kind of organized confusion peculiar to air travel.

Bret rode the escalator up to the second level and checked the Arrivals and Departures schedule. She knew the number of Skip's flight and saw that she had about forty-five minutes to wait.

She walked down the corridor heading to the gate at which the Miami flight was scheduled to arrive.

She was going to surprise Skip. He wasn't aware that she knew this week was his birthday. She'd found out one evening a few weeks ago. She'd met his flight and gone to his condo with him so he could change from his uniform before they went out. While he showered, she'd sneaked a look in his wallet, saw his driver's license and noted his birth date.

That was the same night she'd heard the message on his answering machine from someone called Shelley. The noise of the shower had made it impossible for Skip to hear when the soft voice said, "Call me when you get in, lover, so we can make plans for next weekend." Bret had been shocked at the intimate tone of voice. Quickly she had erased the message.

Right then the idea formed in her head to outsmart that silky voice. She'd planned it all carefully. She'd made reservations at a new and very exclusive restaurant, requesting a secluded table for two. This was a special occasion. Skip's thirty-second birthday.

When a man was over thirty he should start thinking about settling down, stop playing the field. Skip was hoping to make captain, and didn't the airline company look for a stable background for its chief officers flying those superjets?

Bret had for many years taken a dim view of marriage. It had always seemed to be a risky gamble, based on her parents' track records.

But lately it had seemed an appealing alternative to the dead-end life she was leading. She and Skip had lasted longer than some of her other relationships. Maybe she had played her cards right for a change. She hadn't been demanding, she'd given him space…up until now. That voice on the phone posed too big a threat. She felt a twinge of guilt about having erased the message, but all was fair in love and war, right?

In the waiting room she found a seat facing the door through which deplaning passengers would enter from the landing field and the crew would follow a few minutes later.

After a while she opened the magazine she had bought at one of the airport newsstands and flipped through the pages until she found an interesting article. She became so engrossed that she forgot to check her watch. Suddenly the voice over the PA announced the arrival of the Global Airlines Miami flight. She looked up and, after a horde of passengers had de- planed, she saw the crew come through the door. She recognized the flight engineer and Captain Maynard, with whom Skip copiloted.

Then she saw Skip. She closed her magazine and half rose from her chair. She started to wave, then saw that his head was turned from her, looking down into the upturned face of an attractive blond flight attendant.

For a minute Bret couldn't breathe. The two had been totally absorbed in each other, indifferent to the curious and interested glances following them.

Bret felt crushed. So much for surprises. She should have known better.

In a daze Bret canceled the dinner reservations. Could the scene she saw at the airport be easily ex- plained? Skip had told her he often gave one of the flight attendants a ride home from the airport. There was probably nothing to it, nothing serious.

Or was that pretty woman Shelly of the soft drawl?

Maybe Skip would call. But he didn't. Hours passed and her phone didn't ring. It grew dark out- side.

Two days went by with no word from Skip. She knew his schedule, knew when he'd be back in town. She forced herself to make some jewelry presenta- tions to several stores on her call-back list. But she was too distracted, too angry to work, so she came back to her apartment at noon, where she paced, ar- gued with herself and glared at the phone.

She knew she shouldn't do it, but the compulsion was too strong. She dialed Skip's number. Got the message machine. "Skip Dalton here. Sorry but I'm not able to take your call just now. Please leave a message and I'll get back to you as soon as I can."

She hesitated a full minute before the last beep, then her own voice, shaky and almost unrecognizable, said, "Skip, it's me, Bret. I need to talk to you. There's a lot— I mean, I have to talk to you." Suddenly she couldn't seem to stop herself. "Skip, I can't stand this not knowing. I mean, don't do this to me." She hated the way she sounded. But it was too late. Her words were on the tape. If she hadn't seen Skip and that blonde together... But she had. "Please call me when you get in," she finished lamely. She put the phone down and stared at it. She felt like flinging it across the room. Ring! she screamed silently.

Skip's voice sounded weary when he called back. "Rough flight. I'm really tired, Bret. You sounded... well, hysterical. What's up?"

"We need to talk, like I said in my message."

"I don't see that we have all that much to talk about, Bret."

"I think we do." She could almost hear him sigh, see the impatient expression on his face. Recklessly she rushed on. "Skip, I went out to the airport to meet your flight. I saw you and whoever she was."

There was only silence on the other end of the line.

"Skip?" she prompted.

"I don't like being spied on." His voice was harsh.

"I wasn't spying, I thought we were going to see each other—"

"I don't remember anything definite. Anything can happen to change things. There's always the possibility that my flight gets delayed—weather, mechanical— You know I don't like to be quizzed like this, Bret.''

"I'm coming over."

"I don't think that's a good idea."

"I can't take this, Skip. The excuses—"

"Look, Bret—"

"No, you look. I want you to look me in the eye and tell me what's going on."

She hung up and grabbed her car keys, slung her handbag over her shoulder and went out of the apartment. It was now or never.

When Skip opened the door, he was freshly shaved, his hair still damp from a shower. He had on a blue knit sport shirt and gray slacks. He simply nodded, then stepped back so she could enter.

"Can I get you some coffee?" he asked.

"No, I just want to get some things straight."

"I told you this wasn't a good idea, Bret. You're taking a lot for granted, jumping to conclusions—"

"I just want some honest answers."

"I don't like being interrogated." Skip walked into the kitchen, where he poured himself a mug. "Okay, now what do you want to know?"

"Where we're going in this relationship. It's on-again, off-again…you're here then suddenly I can't reach you. You don't return my calls. What am I supposed to do with that?"

"Okay, Bret, but you wanted honesty, remember? I never promised you anything." He took a swallow of his coffee. "Nothing in life is guaranteed. Why can't you just accept that?"

"Because I want something more. I thought you and I had something special."

He put his mug down on the counter and gave her

a long look. "Look, Bret, we had some good times, I'll grant you that. But as for anything more—I'm just not ready to settle down, make a commitment, if that's what you want."

Bret felt the tears stinging her eyes and impatiently blinked them back. She wasn't going to break down here in front of Skip, standing there so cool, so detached. She hated what was happening, didn't want to hear what Skip was saying. She didn't want this to be over. Yet she knew it was.

Still she kept pushing. Her voice was a high-pitched whine and she despised herself for it. "I thought you really cared...."

"Bret, please stop this." Skip frowned. "You're making a scene that's awkward for both of us."

"I thought—" Her voice broke and she couldn't get the words out. What did it matter anyhow?

"If you thought something was happening between us, you were kidding yourself, Bret. A serious relationship is the furthest thing from my mind right now."

"Oh, really?" Bret's tone was sarcastic. "Have you told Shelley that?"

He looked startled.

"Yes, I heard her say 'Call me when you get in, lover.'" She mimicked the soft drawl of the phone voice.

Skip's jaw clenched. "That was pretty low, Bret."

"I guess you might say I was desperate. How long have you and Shelley been an item?"

His mouth straightened into a line. "Two, maybe three months."

"That sounds like pretty long, all at the same time we were—"

Skip's eyes flashed. "You wanted the truth, Bret. I've been trying for weeks to tell you we were through. It didn't take me long to figure out a future was never an option with you. I'd never risk a long-term relationship with a lush."

Rage—hot, burning—flared up in Bret, followed swiftly by crushing humiliation. She drew back her arm and swung, her hand ready to slap his mouth. But Skip caught her wrist and stopped the blow before it landed.

"Okay, you've got that out of your system. Now see if you can sober up."

Her head cleared all of a sudden. It was as if a blinding light had been turned on, and she saw Skip, the situation and herself in the harsh light of truth. She turned and bolted out of the condo, down the outside steps into the parking lot, and got into her car.

She didn't remember backing out, turning around, heading into the stream of traffic. Her mind was empty of all but the seething anger and the awful, scarring sense of rejection.

The word *lush* hammered in Bret's memory as she drove. Her hands gripped the steering wheel. So that was how Skip saw her! How long had he had that opinion?

She thought of the times they had shared cocktails, then had wine with dinner. He was off duty and she had simply been keeping up with him. Or had she? Had she gone on drinking when he'd stopped? Was he observing her and rejecting her while she went on blithely unaware?

She drove, not even noticing that she missed a stop sign and then ran a red light until she heard the whine of a police car siren, saw the flashing lights in her rearview mirror.

Oh, no! She slowed and pulled over to the right. Her heart was pounding, her palms on the steering wheel sweaty. The bulky figure of the policeman stood at her window; she rolled it down.

"May I see your driver's license please, ma'am?" he asked politely.

Bret reached for her handbag, fumbled over her lipstick, a small hairbrush, an earring, before her fingers found her wallet. She took out her license and handed it to the officer. She wasn't sure what he had stopped her for. She was thankful she hadn't been drinking. If she hadn't been so dazed, so distracted by the showdown with Skip, she might have stopped somewhere on her way home. There was every possibility that she could have done that. Thankfully, she had been too upset.

The officer wrote her a ticket for running the Stop sign and red light. She took it with a shaky hand, jammed it into her bag without looking at it. It could have been so much worse. She saw the police car drive off but remained there for a few minutes trying to stop shivering. She closed her eyes and prayed, "Dear God, thank you." She hadn't prayed in a long time, and it seemed self-serving now. But what if she had been drinking? What if she had been arrested as DUI?

Nonie came into her mind. Automatically, Bret whispered, "I'm sorry." She reached for the ignition key and turned it on. Somebody, most probably her grandmother, had been praying for her. "I owe you, Nonie," she said under her breath as she pulled away from the curb and drove slowly and very carefully back to her apartment.

From Lesley to Anne and Bret

I'm leaving to spend the Christmas holidays with my family in Larchmont. I'm in my best friend's wedding on the twenty-ninth. Hope you both have a lovely Christmas.

Anne to Lesley and Bret

I'm planning an old-fashioned Christmas, inviting a few friends for a small party. I'm baking cookies, making cranberry punch—Nonie's recipe—and decorating the house. Wishing you both happy holidays.

E-mail from Bret

Christmas always makes me blue but I'm fighting it. Busy season for the company, lots of gift orders and specials. New Year's looms but I'm not making any resolutions. Never keep them anyway. Cheers!

Chapter Eight

December

At last Anne completed a manuscript that suited Dale. She volunteered to send copies to several publishers of poetry. It was a painstaking, exhausting task, and Anne was glad when all the packages were sent off. She thought she could finally concentrate on her Christmas plans.

But as soon as she handed the postage receipts to Dale, she took on a new role.

Dale was having all kinds of second thoughts about his poems. Anne tried to reassure him, but that just seemed to irritate him further.

All she could do was put up with his increasing moodiness and try to think of ways to cheer him up.

From a few hints Dale had dropped Anne had gathered that his childhood had been less than happy. So with the Christmas vacation coming up, she decided she would create a lovely holiday for them to share.

She would have a tree for them to trim together, presents for Dale to unwrap, a wonderful traditional dinner for her to serve.

With December came the onset of northcoast winter weather. Windy and rainy, one miserable day followed the other. On one such evening Dale came by Anne's house after his class. She noticed right away that something was wrong. He seemed distracted and more restless than usual.

"What's the matter, Dale?" she asked as she took his coat.

"I've put this off as long as I could. I just hated to tell you."

"Hated to tell me what?"

"In September, before I met you, before…before anything had happened with us, I made plans for the Christmas holidays. The same group I traveled with last summer in Europe made reservations at a ski lodge in Colorado. I tried every way to get out of it, but the Lodge won't refund the deposit. A lot of people would lose their money." He threw out his hands in a helpless gesture. "There's no way I can get out of it, Anne. I'm sorry but I've got to go."

Anne thought of all *her* plans, all the preparations *she* had made, the money *she* had spent. She knew it wasn't Dale's fault. Maybe if she'd told him earlier what she wanted to do, there might have been time for him to change his plans. But she had wanted to keep her holiday preparations a surprise. She tried to hide her disappointment. Dale was apologetic, but nothing could be done. It wasn't his fault, she assured him.

On the day before the campus closed down for the holidays, Dale came by her office. He brought out a small, square tissue-wrapped package. It was about the size of a book, Anne noticed. A book of his poems, she could see through the tissue.

"Well, Anne, have a good holiday," he said as he handed it to her. "I'll call you when I get back. Merry Christmas."

She could barely manage a response of "Merry Christmas" to him over the hard lump in her throat. She watched him move through the library, stop to talk to someone, then disappear out the front door.

Not long after that, Anne got her handbag out of her desk drawer, slung her coat over her shoulders and made her way out of the building.

LESLEY

The morning of Terry's wedding Lesley woke up to find the ground covered with a gauzy white layer of snow.

She went down to breakfast in her robe, passing the living room still decorated in its holiday glory, which would remain until after her parents' annual New Year's Eve party.

There was a note on the refrigerator door: "Have gone to get my hair done. Be back at noon. Van wants you to call him. Food in fridge. Eat something!"

Lesley smiled faintly, poured herself a cup of coffee and contemplated the kitchen phone. Van had driven up from Raleigh the night before, and they had talked briefly on the phone then. It had been an unsatisfactory conversation, and Lesley wasn't all that eager to call him.

Since the florist was to deliver flowers to the church, the bridesmaids were to come early to get their bouquets. So it was decided that Van would meet her there.

"Where is Faith and Grace anyway?" he asked. "I can't seem to recall it."

"It's in Weston. You can't miss it. It's a geodesic dome."

"Oh, yeah! Now I know. Near the mill, right?"

For some reason Lesley bristled. Van's tone of voice was so condescending. Exactly the kind her mother used referring to Faith and Grace.

"Why there?"

Lesley tried to keep her voice even. "Because it's where Terry goes when she's in Larchmont. Why else?"

"Just asking. I thought Terry was in the same youth group as the rest of us."

"She was, but she's changed," Lesley said. "That's possible, you know. People *do* change."

Like *me! I've changed.* Not trusting herself to say any more, Lesley cut the call short. "I'll see you there." She hung up feeling irritated and frustrated.

She tried to excuse Van's disparagement of Terry's choice of church. His attitude was no different than her mother's or that of the mother of the bride! Lesley also knew Van was under a great deal of pressure. Passing the bar exam and getting a position with a prestigious law firm were his priorities. If he seemed distracted or indifferent—well, she should overlook it. Shouldn't she? Or did his attitude reflect a drastic gap in the values they each held?

He wasn't even particularly close friends with either Terry or Ben. He had been included in the wedding party because of her.

Lesley finished her coffee and phoned Van at his

mother's house. She was told he'd gone to the club to play racquetball with his old buddy, Greg. Did she want to leave a message?

"No message. I'll see him at the church in a couple of hours."

That got her off the hook. Time enough to tell Van what she knew she must tell him: she had to break the engagement.

Snow continued falling through the afternoon, and by the time Lesley left for the church, the landscape looked like a Christmas card. It seemed appropriate for Terry to have a completely white wedding.

Even with the alterations Vinnie had made at her last fitting, the bridesmaid's gown hung a little loose. Lesley hoped all eyes would be on Terry and no one would notice or remark on her appearance. Before leaving for the wedding, she took off her engagement ring, put it in its box and slipped the box into her handbag. Nobody would notice the ring's absence under her elbow-length gloves. She was determined to return it to Van tonight.

At the church Terry, in her lovely wedding gown, looked beautiful. Her eyes were shining, and her face glowed. Her hair was brushed straight back into a thick braid into which small white flowers were laced.

As the maid of honor Lesley preceded Terry and her father down the aisle. She saw Van standing with the other groomsmen to the left of Ben, whose gaze was centered on his bride.

Lesley tried to smile, but her lips felt stiff and she wasn't sure she managed it. Van's eyes had flickered slightly as she looked at him. Why didn't she feel a rush of happy emotion at seeing him?

While listening to Terry and Ben take their vows,

Lesley knew the answer. She realized she could never make those same promises to Van. Could never mean them or keep them.

It was as simple and as complicated as that.

Lesley felt a swift rush of panic. Her bouquet began to tremble in her suddenly shaky hands. She should have eaten some breakfast or lunch. She'd only had a can of diet cola sometime in the afternoon. Her heart thudded; a pounding began in her temples. She blinked, trying to focus on one of the standing candelabras. Setting her jaw, Lesley willed herself not to faint and spoil Terry's wedding. The pastor was congratulating Terry and Ben, introducing them to the congregation. "I now present the newly married Mr. and Mrs. Ben Hollister."

Terry smiled at Lesley, then took Ben's arm as they went back down the aisle together.

The ceremony was over. Now all she had to do was get through the reception and after that, talk to Van, breaking their engagement. Lesley suppressed a tiny shudder.

Back at the Hollisters' house for the reception, the bridal party gathered to pose for pictures. It seemed to take forever. Lesley felt weaker by the moment. At last the photographer took his final picture and everyone started toward the buffet table.

Lesley found Van. "Do you think you could take me home? I'm not feeling well."

"What? *Now?*" He frowned. "I hardly think we should do that, Les. They haven't even made the toasts yet. I don't think the wedding party is supposed to leave before the bride and groom."

"Yes, I guess you're right," she said, wondering how long she could hold out.

"You do look ghastly pale. Stay put, I'll get you some punch. That should make you feel better."

Van went off, and Lesley found a place to sit down. This was worse than she had expected. She dreaded what she would have to face when she and Van were alone.

When the newlyweds were ready to leave on their honeymoon, Terry aimed her bridal bouquet directly at Lesley. She caught it in a reflex action. Laughter surrounded her, and a chorus of voices teased, "You and Van will be next."

Terry and Ben rushed by in a rain of birdseed. Lesley felt enormous relief. Now they could leave.

"Ready?" Van asked as he came up to her.

"I have my own car here, remember?"

"Okay, well, I'll follow you home."

"Van, I have to talk to you first. Can we sit in your car for a few minutes?"

He looked puzzled. "Can't it wait until we get to your house? It's awfully cold outside."

"No, it can't wait." *I've waited too long already.*

They walked out together. Lesley, still miserably clutching both her own and Terry's bouquets, knew the inevitable moment had come.

Van put her in the passenger side of his car, then got in the other side.

"I'll turn the heater on so we won't freeze while you tell me what's so all-fired important." He sounded irritated.

Lesley opened her envelope bag and felt the square velvet ring box beside her car keys.

"Van, I'm so sorry, but we can't be engaged any longer. I'm giving you your ring back, and I hope one day you'll meet a woman who will love you as you deserve to be loved.''

Of course, Van was stunned. Rejection was a new experience for him, he who had always been the golden boy of Larchmont.

''Is there someone else?'' he demanded.

''No. I just know we're not right for each other, Van. I want to be fair to you.''

''Fair?'' he said curtly. ''Is it something I've done or haven't done?''

''No, I told you, it's not you, it's me. I just don't want to be engaged. That's all.''

Lesley was feeling sicker by the moment. Why couldn't he just accept it, let her go? She didn't want to argue, or explain or hurt him any more.

Finally, she opened the car door and moved to get out. She handed him the ring box. ''Please Van, take this. I'm sorry, truly I am.''

''This is it, then? You really mean it?'' Van asked grimly.

''Yes, Van, I do mean it.''

''I see.'' He pocketed the ring box. ''I guess the verdict's in.''

''Try to understand, Van. I never meant to hurt you.''

In the dim light from the car's dashboard Lesley saw his expression. It held mingled anger, resentment, disbelief. His mouth was set in a straight line.

Lesley hesitated. The snow-flecked wind was chilling her in her light tulle and taffeta dress. She shivered with cold and nerves. ''Goodbye, Van.''

He turned and looked at her. ''I knew there was something wrong. But I didn't know what it was. The problem *is* you, Lesley,'' he snapped.

She started to close the car door when he shouted, "You'd better do something about yourself. You look like a skeleton. Whatever you're on must be doing something to your brain as well as your looks."

Harsh words, but Lesley realized he was speaking out of his own wounded pride, his anger and resentment.

She knew she'd hurt him. But she also knew Van would not nurse this hurt long. He was too attractive, too resourceful, too healthy.

As she hurried over to her own car, she heard him speed away. She was shaking so, she could hardly get the key in the ignition. But at least she had done it, she said to herself as she drove home. She should feel free. Instead, she was furious that Van had thought she was "on" something. If she could find something that would make things okay, her life all right, she would certainly be "on" it. As it was, she only had the deep, aching void inside where nothing could reach, nothing could help. An emptiness that nothing—not even food—could fill.

BRET

Bret walked down the street and over two blocks to the liquor store.

Inside was a young man standing behind the counter talking to another guy. They glanced in her direction, then went back to their conversation. She knew that she looked like a wreck in her sweats, with no makeup. She hadn't even bothered to comb her hair. It hadn't seemed to matter. Nothing had seemed to matter much for weeks—not since that awful scene with Skip. She kept hearing his sarcastic voice in her head: "I'd never risk a long-term relationship with a lush."

She walked over to the shelves stocked with various wines. All she needed was a half-gallon of one of the cheaper brands. Anything with enough alcohol content to dull the pain so she could go to sleep, stop obsessing about Skip.

While she stood there mindlessly reading labels, one of the clerks looked over at her curiously.

"Can I help you with anything, miss?" he asked.

"I...Well, I'm having some people over and I can't decide what kind of wine to get," she said vaguely. Of course it was a lie. She saw the two clerks exchange a knowing glance. Her cheeks burned.

"Well, it depends, ma'am. Are you having meat or fish? That usual rule of thumb is red for meat, white for fish." His tone was tinged with sarcasm. He knew she was bluffing.

She grabbed three bottles of white zinfandel off the shelf and took them over to the counter. The clerk began to ring them up. "That'll be—" he named the amount.

That would take all the cash she had with her. She hesitated. "Can I write a check?"

"Local?" he asked frowning.

She nodded. She wasn't sure what her balance was. She'd let the statements pile up for the last two months without opening them, simply banking her paycheck as she received it, using her credit card most of the time. Irresponsible, that snide little voice in her head remarked. She wrote the check for ten dollars more than the bill. The clerk gave her the change, then bagged the three bottles of wine. She saw something in his eyes as she picked up the sack. Contempt? Something that said, "You're not fooling me, lady."

Walking back to her apartment, she told herself it didn't matter. When she'd finished the wine, Christmas would be over. Oblivion. That was all she really wanted.

Chapter Nine

December and January

Late in the afternoon two days before Christmas, fog was quickly rolling in. It swirled around the lampposts veiling the redwoods surrounding the campus and obliterating even the closest houses on Anne's street. Although all her plans had vanished like so much smoke, Anne agreed with Dickens's famous suggestion that no matter what, "Christmas should be kept," and she intended to keep it.

Determined not to be depressed because she was spending Christmas alone, Anne put on some of her favorite Christmas music, lit the red candles on the mantel and heated cranberry juice with a teaspoon of lemon and several cinnamon sticks.

The mingled aromas of simmering cranberry punch, scented bayberry candles and the spicy fragrance of the small but beautifully shaped cedar tree

Anne had selected with so much care almost
mocked her.

She had thought that Dale would be spending many
evenings here with her during the Christmas vacation.
With that in mind she had mixed up a batch of cookie
batter and refrigerated it to bake later. A fun project
to do together. Or maybe too domestic? Perhaps she
had been wrong about her relationship with Dale. The
carefree bachelor was much more likely to enjoy a
holiday on the ski slopes than celebrating cozily in
her parlor.

Activity was always the antidote for self-pity or
loneliness, Anne told herself, and got busy in the
kitchen. Humming to herself along with the familiar
Christmas music she had on her tape recorder, she
rolled out the cookie dough. She had just put the last
batch into the oven when her doorbell pealed.

She wiped her hands on a kitchen towel and went
to the front door. To her startled surprise Elliott Grayson and Maddie were standing on the porch.

"We're stranded," Elliott said with a sheepish
grin. "The airport is shut down, all flights canceled.
Highway 201 is closed. I can't drive Maddie to San
Francisco to catch her flight from there. It looks as
though the Grinch stole Christmas. I'm holding out
for some kind of Christmas miracle, though."

"Come in," Anne invited, stepping back and opening the door wider. Maddie's knitted cap had slipped
sideways, and she looked like one of those Kean
paintings of wide-eyed waifs.

As they stepped into the hall, Elliott said, "I could
barely see two feet ahead of me driving from the airport where we got the bad news."

"Oh, you've got a tree!" exclaimed Maddie.

"Yes," Anne said, helping Maddie off with her jacket.

"I didn't get one." Elliott explained. "I didn't think Maddie would be with me, and somehow a tree seemed...I don't know...." He left the rest unfinished.

Maddie turned to Anne, a hopeful note in her voice. "And it isn't decorated."

"So you can help me."

"Oh, great. Can we, Daddy?"

"I guess so. That is, if it's okay with Anne if we stay a while?" He looked at Anne. "Unexpected company is not always welcome."

"It is in this house." She smiled at him. "I believe in what the Scripture reminds us, 'Be not forgetful to entertain strangers: for thereby some have entertained angels unaware.'" She always loved that verse from Hebrews 13:2.

Maddie giggled. "Anne called us angels, Daddy."

"Well, I don't know about that. Actually I don't mean to impose on your hospitality for long, Anne. Could I use your phone? I need to get in touch with Valerie. Let her know what's happened. She was supposed to meet Maddie's plane in Chicago."

"Of course. You can use the phone in the kitchen," Anne told him. "Meanwhile Maddie and I will get out the ornaments and start trimming the tree. How does that sound?"

Elliott went out to the kitchen, and Maddie said, "I'm a UAM."

"What's that?"

"Unaccompanied minor. That's airline jargon. I'm put on the flight in one place and someone else meets me at the other end. Daddy or Mommy, whoever's turn it is to have me.''

Anne felt a little pang of sympathy for a child being bounced back and forth from one parent to the other. Not an ideal childhood, for sure.

''Well, let's get out the ornaments and go to work on the tree,'' she suggested, and Maddie happily agreed.

''My mother's been married three times,'' the child remarked casually. Or at least it seemed she had thrown it out without any particular emotion. It was, however, a real conversation stopper. What kind of a reply was Anne supposed to make to that?

Elliott came out of the kitchen. ''Your mother's disappointed, Maddie, but we'll keep in touch. And as soon as the weather permits, we'll see if we can get you on the next flight.''

''Okay.'' Maddie's reply was nonchalant as she busily sorted through the beaded ropes of glitter in the box of trimmings. Was she used to sudden changes of plans?

Anne looked up from the string of tree lights she was untangling as Elliott came back into the room. ''Have you eaten?''

He frowned. ''We were going to stop at McDonald's for a hamburger, but we didn't get that far.''

''I have cream of chicken soup I can heat.''

''Well, I hate to put you to any trouble. We've already inconvenienced you enough, barging in like this.''

''Not at all, Elliott. Actually I'm glad for the company.'' She got up from the floor. ''Honestly I am,'' she assured him when he still looked doubtful.

As she heated the soup, she sliced the loaf of buttered French bread, sprinkled it with Parmesan cheese and slid it under the broiler. She was glad she had baked the cookies after all. Christmas cookies, with the maple pecan ice cream, ought to make a dandy dessert for an impromptu supper.

As it turned out the meal was lively and happy, and afterward the three of them had fun trimming the tree.

"This is the prettiest tree I've ever seen. Don't you think so, Daddy?" Maddie asked as she carefully smoothed a last skein of tinsel on a bough.

"Let's see how it looks with the lights on," Anne suggested and bent to push in the plug. There was a brief moment of glory, which they greeted with prolonged oohs, then suddenly the lights went out and they were left in complete darkness.

"Uh-oh, did we blow a fuse?" Anne gasped.

"No," Elliott said looking out the window. "The whole street is out. Maybe some driver hit one of the light poles in the fog."

"Well, don't worry, I've got lots of candles. We can use them until whatever the problem is gets fixed. I guess the road crews are out in force on a night like this." Anne was glad that she had bought extra candles.

She groped her way to the table where she had put them away and then into the kitchen for matches. Soon candles were burning everywhere, glowing warmly. The lovely scent of bayberry mingled with that of cedar, and the house was filled with soft light and fragrance.

"I like it this way," Maddie said. Her little round face, illuminated by the candle glow, looked happy.

Somehow in the last few hours it had lost that pinched look of anxiety she'd had when she first arrived.

Anne placed another log on the fire, and a spiral of sparks flew upward. Maybe this was how the parlor had looked on a long-ago Christmas evening when the original owners had celebrated the holidays in the 1880s.

Maddie was curled up at one end of the love seat facing the tree. "Last year Mommy had a pink tree," Maddie said to no one in particular, yawning.

Elliott stood up. "We should be on our way. I'm afraid we're imposing on Anne."

Anne glanced at Maddie, whose eyelids were fluttering and slowly closing. "Not at all. Why not stay here, Elliott? Maddie is almost asleep, and this is nearer the airport in case the weather clears tomorrow and she can get out."

He hesitated. "It seems like such an imposition."

"I wish you wouldn't keep on like that. You two have made my Christmas," she told him. Then, a little embarrassed by perhaps revealing too much, she said quickly, "Look, it would be a shame to disturb Maddie. She can sleep right there until morning. And the couch converts into a bed. I don't think you'd be too uncomfortable."

"That's very kind of you, Anne, but—"

"Elliott, stop fussing." She went over to Maddie, gently removed the little girl's glasses, putting them on the table beside the love seat, then drew an afghan over her. "She's out like a light."

"You are awfully kind, Anne."

"Nonsense, it's been a wonderful evening. I would have been here alone if you two hadn't shown up.

Now, let's have a cup of cider and enjoy the fire." She smiled and moved toward the kitchen.

When she returned, he had placed several large pillows on the floor in front of the fireplace.

Elliott looked over at her. In the firelight her hair was the rich color of amber-honey and her skin had a delicate rosy tint.

"Do you believe in fate, Anne?" he asked.

"I don't know. I guess it depends on what you mean by fate."

"Are the events of our lives just chance, coincidence, happenstance? Or do you think everything in our lives is predestined, preordained?"

"I think when we look back we may see some sort of pattern. I hardly think we're aware of it when it's happening."

"Doesn't it strike you as strange that we both came here to Glenharbor, met at this particular time in our lives?"

Where was this leading? Anne wondered.

"That's a little deep for me."

"Maybe, but on the other hand, what other explanation is there?"

"For what?"

"I sometimes have the feeling I've known you before, a kind of—" He chuckled. "As Yogi Berra would say, 'déjà vu all over again.'"

Maybe Elliott was right, Anne mused. Maybe a person didn't recognize those special moments in life. She gave him a searching look. She knew instinctively that this was a man of strength and character, who took his responsibilities seriously. Especially those of being a father.

She felt a stirring within her, as though something

wonderful was on the brink of happening. Was this one of those defining moments in life? She wanted to recognize it if it was. But then again, she had been wrong before.

Anne became aware of Elliott watching her. Was he waiting for her to say something? She was afraid that, in this magical atmosphere, she might say or do something she'd regret. She got to her knees, then stood up.

"It's getting late. I'll get you some pillows and blankets."

She went upstairs quickly and brought them back.

"Thanks again, Anne," Elliott said. "You've been more than generous."

"It's been my pleasure, Elliott. Maddie's a dear. I've enjoyed having you both."

They said good-night. Then Anne went to bed…but not immediately to sleep.

She woke to the smell of bacon frying and the aroma of coffee. At first she thought she must be dreaming. Then she heard voices and remembered. Elliott and Maddie. She hurriedly pulled on jeans and a sweater and went downstairs.

Elliott turned around from where he stood at the stove grinning.

"Good thing yours is a gas stove. The electricity's still off. Hope you don't mind that I took over here. Thought the least I could do was make breakfast." He held the spatula in one hand. "How do you like your eggs?"

"Whatever you two are having is fine. Good morning, Maddie." She smiled at the little girl, who smiled back shyly.

"I set the table. I hope it's okay."

"Wow, I'm not used to such service. Yes, it's fine, just right."

Elliott paused from whipping eggs to say, "By the way, I called the airport. San Francisco is operational. I got Maddie a flight."

"That's good," Anne said, looking at his daughter. Was she mistaken, or did a shadow of disappointment cross the child's face?

After they ate, Anne brushed Maddie's hair for her and tied it back with a red satin ribbon she had used when wrapping her Christmas gifts.

"All set?" Elliott asked standing at the front door with Maddie's duffel bag and suitcase.

"Yes, Daddy," Maddie said, putting on her tam. Then, turning to Anne, she said in a small voice, "It was nice being here."

"It was nice having you," Anne replied, truly meaning it.

How truly she didn't realize until after Elliott's car had disappeared down the hill. The house seemed deadly quiet and empty.

So as not to let Christmas pass completely unobserved, Anne attended the midnight candlelight service at the community church. Somehow her thoughts kept returning to the picture of Maddie, the UAM, fastened into her seat on the jet winging toward Chicago, and of Elliott, alone now after seeing his daughter off.

Anne to Bret and Lesley
My Christmas plans didn't work out the way I expected. But I had surprise visitors and it really turned out to be a lovely time.

Lesley to Anne and Bret

My big news this New Year is that I broke my engagement to Van. I finally came to the conclusion I wasn't ready and he wasn't the one. Stunned everyone in Larchmont but I know it was the right thing to do.

No word from Bret

BRET

Two days later Bret woke up with heavy-lidded eyes, a dry mouth and a booming headache. The red light on her telephone was flashing. Groggily she groped for the Play button and pressed it. There were several messages from Linda Mercer, her supervisor. Bret listened to them in a buzz, wincing as the voice got more irritated with each recorded message. "Please return this call, Bret. It's important. I'm getting reports from customers not being serviced. I'd like some answers."

Brett shuddered. What could she say? *I've been drowning my sorrows over another botched romance.* That would go over big with Linda, the ultimate career woman.

Even though Bret knew it was bound to happen, felt it coming, knew she deserved it, being fired came as a shock.

Linda, chicly coiffed and fashionably dressed for success, spoke in a crisp, no-nonsense manner. "I'm sorry, Bret, but your sales have fallen below the minimum we've established for our reps. I've extended you more than the usual time we allot when one of our reps fails to meet her quotas, to allow for possible personal problems that might account for the sudden slump in sales. But your record has been below average for too long now." Linda tapped her pen on the glass-topped desk in a rapid staccato. "Maybe you need some time off. Or maybe you need a change of pace. I'm certainly willing to consider reinstatement at some time in the future." Linda paused and pursed her lips. "We regret having to let you go, but after all, business is business."

Bret tried not to show what a blow this was.

"Yes, of course, I understand." Somehow she managed to maintain a semblance of composure as she said goodbye to Linda and left the office.

Bret knew at some level she had been waiting for it to happen. Now it had. So now what?

On her way to her apartment, she stopped to fill her gas tank. As she handed her credit card to the service station clerk, she wondered if this would be the last time she could use it. She used to put her gas purchases on her expense account. Pulling out into traffic, she drove mindlessly, automatically shifting, changing lanes. She should make some plans. But her mind was blank. Being fired was a new experience. Usually it was she who quit a job. No matter how warranted her firing was, it did severe damage to her self-esteem.

When she reached her apartment, Bret was wired tight. Luckily, she had gone to the grocery store over the weekend and had enough food on hand. Enough liquor. Good thing, because if ever she needed a drink, it was now.

Chapter Ten

January

The Tuesday after New Year's, classes resumed. The campus came back to life. Back at work, Anne kept watching the library entrance from her half-open office door, wondering how soon Dale would come by to see her.

It was nearly four o'clock when she saw him enter the building. He looked great—tanned, trim. He was wearing a handsome gray sweater, obviously hand-knit. At the door of her office he greeted her with a brilliant smile.

"Happy New Year." He brought one hand out from behind his back and held out a single red rose.

Anne tried to be casual.

"Well, hello, stranger. Don't you look spiffy?"

"Busy tonight?" Dale's question corralled Anne's thoughts back to the present. She shook her head.

"Ronzoni's?"

"That would be nice," she answered. "What time will you pick me up?"

He hesitated. "Could you meet me there? I have a meeting scheduled with Mitzi Alton, who's going to be directing the drama department's production of *The Belle of Amherst.*" He shrugged. "Say, around seven?"

"Okay, fine." Anne felt let down. She had pictured their reunion differently.

When she got to the restaurant, she was even further dismayed. Mitzi Alton and Hugh Bennett, both from the drama department, were seated at the table with Dale. Dale hadn't mentioned they were joining them. Mitzi gave Anne a cool, appraising glance. Dale told her he had already ordered for them and hoped it was okay. Anne sat down. Their food came, and the others continued their conversation.

Anne had not finished eating when Dale looked at his watch and announced, "We better get over to the theater. Rehearsal starts in ten minutes."

Bennett rose, too, mumbling something of an apology to Anne.

"Sorry, Anne," Dale said, standing up. At least he had the grace to look embarrassed.

"It's okay. I understand." Actually she thought they had all behaved badly. When she finished her meal and the waiter came to remove their plates, she noticed no one had left a tip. She dug into her wallet and drew out several bills.

Fuming with outrage not only about how they had treated *her* but their indifference to the students working at the restaurant, Anne left and went out to her car.

To her surprise, in the parking lot she saw Mitzi. "Anne, over here," she called.

Puzzled, since she assumed Mitzi had gone with the men, Anne walked toward her.

Mitzi wasted no time getting to the point.

"I just wanted you to know that Dale and I are in a relationship." Her words were spoken flatly. "I thought it was only fair you should know. Dale's kept putting off telling you that whatever you had is over."

Anne was speechless. Not knowing how to respond, she simply turned and went to her own car, got in and drove away.

When Anne got home, she tossed off her coat, dropped her handbag and went upstairs. Without turning on the lights, she lay down on the bed.

What a fool she had been. Not to see how very self-centered Dale really was. Not to accept that their relationship—more precisely his fling with her—was over.

She had ignored the signs even though they were pretty clear. His brief span of interest in her had run its course. Her time as Dale's muse had been short-lived. Actually he had used her. She thought of the hours she had spent getting his poetry ready for submission.

It didn't take long to confirm that what Mitzi had said was true. Dale's late-night calls stopped. His drop-by visits after jogging came to a halt. When Anne happened to run into him on campus, he greeted her with his usual enthusiasm but was always in a hurry. "Gotta run, Anne, on my way to a meeting." Or, "Wish we could chat but I'm running late."

Finally she realized she wanted to tell someone about it, and she called Nada.

"You sound rather upset, Anne. What's troubling you?"

Anne recounted the episode with Mitzi.

"Well, I know the man has a gigantic ego. You're much better off without him."

"I feel pretty foolish."

"I wouldn't give it another thought, Anne," Nada said dismissively and abruptly changed the subject. "How is Elliott Grayson?"

"Actually we spent some time together at Christmas," Anne replied, hoping Nada wouldn't make too much of that. She quickly explained what had happened.

"Nice man." Nada smiled. "And have you been seeing him since?"

Guiltily Anne recalled several messages Elliott had left on her answering machine that she had not returned. She had been trying to heal the wounds made by Dale Myers in her heart.

There was a significant pause on the line, then Nada asked, "Did you take my suggestion about prayer, Anne? Try it, if you haven't. It's the only advice I give that I'm sure has backup."

After they hung up, Anne realized she hadn't prayed much lately. She needed to remember how much Nonie believed in praying about everything.

But that night as she lay in bed all Anne could think about was the bad decisions she'd constantly made, how she'd set herself up yet again for heartbreak, by choosing the wrong man.

"Oh, Anne," she said to herself through the tears, "when will you ever learn?"

LESLEY

Ever since Christmas in Larchmont, Lesley's emotions had been in turmoil. She had known breaking her engagement wouldn't be easy, but she had not guessed it would be this awful. Her parents' reaction might have been expected: her mother was appalled, her father silent, though he obviously thought she'd made a mistake.

"Bad as that, huh?" Lesley's friend and fellow teacher, Donna, had said when Lesley told her what had happened.

"Yes, but I know I did the right thing."

"Well, that's what matters, Les."

Back in the demanding routine of her teaching job Lesley had suffered more dizzy spells and overwhelming fatigue.

Now in Dr. Bates's reception room, Lesley tapped her foot impatiently. She was here under pressure. She had put off making a doctor's appointment until that fainting spell at a teachers' meeting had cinched it. They had rushed her to the emergency room. Everyone at school was concerned. After that she couldn't make any excuses.

Lesley sighed, picked up a fashion magazine from the assortment and flipped indifferently through its glossy pages. She checked her watch. Her appointment was for two-thirty; it was now three-fifteen. She looked around the room filled with other waiting patients. As a general practitioner, the doctor would have a busy practice with all kinds of cases, but still....

The office door opened and a young man on crutches entered. He maneuvered himself into a chair and sat down with some difficulty, stretching out his leg, which was immobilized in a plaster cast, and wedging his crutches between his and the next chair.

He was outdoorsy looking, tanned and with tousled sandy hair. He also looked vaguely familiar. He caught Lesley's gaze and there seemed to be a flicker of awareness in his. She realized she must have been staring and went back to her magazine, trying to think where she had seen him before.

Just then a nurse came to the door of the reception room. "Ladies and gentlemen, I'm sorry but the doctor has been delayed at the hospital by an emergency. I'm afraid he'll be a while getting here. Those of you who want to reschedule your appointment are welcome to do so. Others may want to wait it out, but I can't say just how long it might be."

Lesley decided now that she was here she might as well wait it out. She glanced at the guy on crutches. He grinned. "I'm getting my cast off today, so I'm not going anywhere until that's done." He whipped a pocket-size leather book from his jacket pocket. "Anyway, I've got a good book to read." He held it up so she could read the title—*Mere Christianity,* by C. S. Lewis.

Interesting choice for someone who was obviously athletic, Lesley thought. A seminary student? A minister? Should she ask? She really didn't want to get involved in a conversation, though. She had too much on her mind. So she simply nodded and returned to her magazine.

Finally the nurse came to the door leading to the inner offices and said, "Jeff Scott?" She smiled. "We know what you're here for. You can come in now."

The young man hefted himself up on his crutches and chuckled. "I'm ready."

The nurse held the door so he could go through,

then turned to Lesley. "Miss Sherwood?" Reluctantly Lesley rose and followed the white-uniformed figure down the hallway to one of the examining rooms.

A few minutes later she sat on the edge of the examining room table shivering in the flimsy paper gown.

The door of the examining room opened, and a man in a white lab coat, a stethoscope dangling out of one pocket, a clipboard in his hand, entered the examining room.

"Miss Sherwood?" he said matter-of-factly. "I'm Dr. Bates. You were referred by Dr. Collier to my associate, who is out of town. I'm seeing his referrals. Ones that are urgent."

"Oh, I'm not urgent," Lesley assured him.

"No?" He looked up from her chart.

Under his steady gaze Lesley felt her face get hot. He looked down at the clipboard he was holding again.

"It says here that you fainted and were brought into the emergency room at General Hospital, where you were kept overnight for observation. That sounds urgent to me." A brief smile touched his strong mouth. "Let's take a look and see what's going on."

He did a complete, thorough exam. When he finished marking the vials containing the blood he had drawn from her arm, he looked at her sternly. "Now take a walk across the room for me, please," he directed briskly.

She slid off the table and started toward the door over the shiny vinyl floor. She wobbled and lost her balance and had to steady herself by reaching out for a chair.

"Uh-huh." Dr. Bates wrote something on the chart. He helped her back up on the table, then made another notation.

"Well, we'll have to wait to get the test results back from the lab to be sure, but I think I can safely tell you that you're on the verge of a serious complication from an eating disorder."

"Eating disorder?" Lesley gasped.

He met her startled gaze.

"That's what your body is trying to tell you. You better start eating normally, young lady, or you're going to be in big trouble."

"But I do eat. Very healthfully. I try to be careful—"

"Careful not to gain weight? Maybe you don't know that drastic weight loss and excessive dieting can lead to heart failure and sudden death?"

"Are you trying to scare me?"

"I hope that does scare you. But, no, I'm just warning you." Dr. Bates looked at her chart. "Ninety-one pounds is not nearly enough for someone five foot five." He clicked his ballpoint pen and replaced it in his pocket. "You need to be hospitalized and in a supervised food-monitoring program for a time."

"Hospital?" Lesley was shocked. "Surely I can put on some weight without going to a hospital!"

"The question is, will you?"

"I'm a very disciplined person," Lesley said defensively. "If I have to do something, I do it."

"No question of that, Miss Sherwood. You'd have to be very disciplined indeed to starve yourself to this degree. I see I haven't made myself clear. You're in a danger zone. You need help. I can't force you, but

I strongly recommend you follow my advice and let me check you into the hospital.''

Dr. Bates waited for her answer. Lesley nervously fingered the silver cross that hung on a chain around her neck. A thoughtful expression passed over his face.

''Are you a Christian, Miss Sherwood?''

''Why, y-yes,'' she stammered, wondering what that had to do with her decision.

Dr. Bates moved to the door. ''I'm just wondering if this is some radical cult thing, some form of penance? For your sake, I hope you haven't distorted religion. My advice to you, Miss Sherwood is get help. Preferably psychological.'' With that the doctor went out of the room, letting the heavy door swing shut behind him.

Lesley's hands were shaking as she got dressed.

Dr. Bates was standing at the nurses' station when she came out of the examining room. He looked up questioningly at her approach.

''I'm going to take your advice, put on some weight.'' She smiled.

''That wasn't my advice, Miss Sherwood, but if you decide to ignore what I really said, well—'' He shrugged. ''I'll send my recommendation to Dr. Collier.''

''Thank you. I do appreciate your concern. And I will remember what you said.''

He gave her a curt nod, turned and walked back down the hall to his office. Feeling as rebuffed as a child, she peered over the counter at the nurses' station and saw her chart. By bending her neck a little she was able to read the line, ''Diagnosis: Anorexia

Nervosa," and on the line under that "Prognosis: Poor."

Lesley left the doctor's office and walked out into the cold January afternoon, chilled and more than a little frightened.

BRET

Bret had not been out of her apartment for a week. She sat on the couch, turned on the TV and, clicker in hand surfed for the channel that showed reruns of old sitcoms like *The Mary Tyler Moore Show.*

Bret wanted the charmed life that Mary had. A fantasy existence where all the problems were solved in a half hour with time out for commercials.

Bret noticed that her wineglass was empty, so she went out to the kitchen to get a refill.

A calendar hung on the back of the cabinet door she opened to take out the wine bottle. Bret looked at it in astonishment. Had it really been three weeks since she had been fired? Another week and her rent would be due. She suppressed a shudder. She poured her wine and went back into the living room. She settled back on the sofa and continued to surf until she found an episode of *The Mary Tyler Moore Show.* The scene was Mary's apartment, and she and Rhoda were talking about…something. Bret lost track of the plot as her thoughts turned to her own situation.

Out of a job, nowhere to be, no one to report to, no one to care about where she was or what she was doing. Maudlin! For Pete's sake, was she becoming a crying drunk? She clicked off the remote and went out to the kitchen.

More bad news. She didn't have enough coffee to make a full pot. Of all days when she needed some desperately. Much as she didn't feel like it, she'd have to go out and buy some.

She pulled on sweats and running shoes and grabbed her wallet and keys and went out the door. The morning air had just enough briskness to give it a snap. Maybe she should start jogging, get in shape.

Good News Brew was at the corner. The interior was fragrant with all the different coffee blends they sold. She'd have a cup here and buy a pound of their special beans to take home.

Bret got her coffee, moved to a table where someone had left a morning paper and sat down. Her coffee spilled a little as she set it down, and she grabbed a paper napkin to wipe it up. It was then she noticed the words printed on the napkin: "Wake up and smell the coffee." It hit her. "That's exactly what I should do." Take a good hard look at her life and where it was going. She didn't want to keep repeating her mistakes. What was the root of all the disorder she felt? The restlessness, the dissatisfaction.

Psychologists say everything that's visible in our adult lives has its source in our childhood. But had hers been any more dysfunctional than most people's? All you had to do was tune into *Montel Williams* or *Oprah* or *Judge Judy* to see it hadn't.

She was smart enough, Bret told herself. She should be able to figure out the underlying reason for her problems. For the dissatisfaction that drove her to change jobs so often. Change men. Change environments. The constant need for something new. After the first excitement, suddenly her enthusiasm would drop, her interest dim. She'd begin to find things wrong with the man, the job, the apartment. Nothing seemed to last with her. How did anyone find contentment, fulfillment, enduring love?

Well, she didn't need to be hit over the head with a two-by-four. She knew the problems; now she should try to find some answers.

Why not take her week at Spindrift now? She could drive to Greenbrae, get the keys from Bernessa. Maybe that was why Nonie had left the cottage to them with the requirement that they each spend a week alone there. What better place to try to figure her life out?

Part III

Chapter Eleven

January and February

The two-lane road to Sea Watch Cove was a long, flat stretch bound on one side by tall lolly pines and on the other by the barely visible rim of blue ocean beyond the sand dunes.

Bret wasn't sure what she would get from this week alone. *I've made such a mess of my life. But I'm going to try to put it together. Some way. Somehow.*

The closer she got to Sea Watch Cove and Spindrift, the more memories of Nonie came to mind. Bret knew Nonie would have been terribly disappointed at the disarray of her granddaughter's life. She had always had so much faith and trust in Bret, Anne and Lesley. Well, maybe during this week at the cottage Bret could somehow absorb some of Nonie's own view of life, regain some balance.

It began to drizzle as she made the turn onto the

beach road. Clouds hung heavy and dark, and the pewter-colored ocean looked angry.

It didn't take long for Bret to settle in at Spindrift. She hadn't brought much. Her main idea was to get out to the beach, get some sun, collect her thoughts, make some plans, some decisions about the future. But if the foul weather continued, she wondered how she would spend her time.

Tired from the long drive, she went to bed early. The next morning she went down to the kitchen and made herself instant coffee.

A survey of the kitchen cabinets made clear that she needed to shop for food. She went to Dennison's Giant Superette where she bought bread, coffee, butter, eggs and a couple of cans of soup. She hesitated at the liquor shelves, then put a couple of bottles of wine in her basket. A little vino would ease some of the tension, help her think about the future. Even the Bible said "Wine maketh the heart merry." Or was that Shakespeare? Either way, Bret reasoned, she needed a little relaxation after all the emotional trauma of her breakup with Skip and losing her job.

It was beginning to rain hard by the time Bret reached the cottage. She dried herself off and had a quick supper of cheese, bread and two glasses of wine. When she was finished, Bret found herself restless, but it was too early to go to bed.

Nonie had never had a television at Spindrift. Bad reception was her explanation. At first the girls, used to spending hours in front of the tube, were at a loss as to what to do when the weather kept them from their usual beach pursuits. Nonie had introduced them to different board games—Chinese checkers, Monopoly, Scrabble. And jigsaw puzzles. Nonie always played with such enthusiasm that soon the girls did not even miss TV. But being here alone was different. Bret prowled the cottage.

She rejected the temptation to while the evening away with some more wine. But she needed some entertainment. Then she spotted the row of old novels in the bookshelf. She recalled seeing Nonie engrossed in a certain book one summer. What was the title? Bret's index finger ran across the spines of books on the shelf, searching for it. Seeing *The Robe,* she stopped and pulled it out. The pages were slightly yellowed; some even dog-eared, as if Nonie had been interrupted at this point and, lacking a bookmark, had folded the page at the top corner. If Nonie had enjoyed *The Robe* so much, maybe she would, too, Bret decided.

But just in case her first choice didn't hold her attention she picked out a few more books—*Magnificent Obsession, Green Dolphin Street*—and set them on the coffee table in front of the studio couch. Then wrapping one of Nonie's afghans around her and bunching some of the throw pillows behind her head, she curled up and began to read.

The setting of *The Robe* was ancient Rome, in which she had never been very interested, yet Bret was surprised to find herself caught up in the compelling story. She only moved once, to pour herself a glass of wine, then came back to read some more. Suddenly she was startled by a knock at the door. She flung aside the afghan, and glass in hand went to answer it.

A man stood there, wearing a windbreaker with the collar turned up. "Hi there, I'm Reid Martin. I live a little way down the beach on the other side of the road. I just got back from a business trip and saw the lights on here. I knew Spindrift had been empty since last summer, so I just thought I'd come by and check. See if everything was okay. We year-rounders have a 'good neighbor' policy to look after each other.''

He was good-looking, with nicely molded features and a strong jawline. There were deep lines in his tanned face and lots of crinkly laugh lines around his eyes. It was a good face, Bret thought.

"I'm Bret Sherwood," she introduced herself. "I'm just down here for a few days. My cousins and I inherited my grandmother's cottage. She died last year."

"Yes, I know. I'm sorry. I didn't know her well. We were beach acquaintances—passed each other walking, waved, said good morning, that sort of thing. Of course, everyone in Sea Watch Cove spoke highly of her.''

"She was quite a lady." Bret stepped back, holding the door open. "Won't you come in?"

"Thanks. That is, if I'm not interrupting anything?"

"I was reading, that's all. Come in." She opened the door wider and he stepped inside. She held up her glass. "Join me?"

"No, thanks."

"Coffee?"

"I've never been known to turn down a cup of coffee. Old navy habit, I guess." He unzipped his jacket and hung it over the back of one of the straight chairs.

"You were in the navy?"

"Yes, for a few years."

Bret went into the kitchen and poured each of them a mug of coffee.

Reid picked up one of the books on the coffee table and held it up. "You reading this?"

Bret came back into the front room and saw the title. "*Magnificent Obsession?* No. Why?"

"I just wondered because—" He paused and took the mug of coffee she handed him "—several years ago I saw this book in a stall of used books at one of those street fairs. A paperback edition. I remember seeing the blurb printed diagonally across the cover: 'This book might just change your life.' The price was fifty cents. The person I was with remarked, 'How can something that costs fifty cents change your life?'" Reid looked up from the book he was holding and smiled. "But it did."

"Change your life?"

"In a way." Reid took a sip of coffee. "In a very profound way, actually."

Bret was curious, but did not feel she knew Reid Martin well enough to ask him how the book had affected him. Instead, she said, "All these books belonged to my grandmother. I just picked one at random." She pointed to *The Robe,* which she had laid facedown when she answered the door.

"Coincidentally, I just saw it on TV last week," Reid said. "A very powerful story."

"I thought I might find it boring, but I can't put it down."

While Reid drank his coffee, they talked—mainly about Sea Watch Cove and how it was threatened by big developers who wanted to change it into a mini-Miami Beach.

"What are you and your cousins planning to do with Spindrift?" Reid inquired.

"We haven't decided yet. We all have such different lives. Both my cousins will meet me here at the end of the summer and we'll make our decision then."

"I hope you decide to keep it. And if you do, join the rest of us homeowners here to fight the developers. Sea Watch Cove is special and shouldn't be lost." Reid put down his coffee mug and got to his feet. "Well, thanks very much for the coffee and the hospitality, Bret. I shouldn't have barged in uninvited like this. But as I said, I was concerned. There aren't many of us here at this time of year."

"Thanks for being a good neighbor." Bret smiled as she walked to the door with him.

What a genuinely nice guy, Bret thought after Reid Martin left. How was it she'd never met anyone like that before? Well, maybe she hadn't looked in the right places. You didn't find that type in a hotel bar.

She thought of the dozens of dimly lit bars she had gone into on her trips, seeking…what? A conversation, someone to heal the constant loneliness? Usually she turned down the offer of a drink, did not return the tentative smile of a stranger. Sometimes she had accepted and regretted it. It didn't help, it never had. Bret read till she was sleepy, then went to bed.

She awoke to an overcast morning. A light, steady rain was falling.

Bret bundled up in a warm sweater, curled up on the sofa and started reading *The Robe* again. As the day wore on, the only sounds were the drip of the rain and the turning of page after page. She got up once to make a pot of coffee and get some corn chips, then it was back to the sofa and the book.

It was early in the afternoon when she saw that it had stopped raining. She put the book down, got up and stretched and decided to take a walk on the beach to get some fresh air. Putting on a warm jacket and scarf, she set out.

The beach was empty, the sand dark and damp from the steady rain. A few seagulls wheeled overhead, dipping and diving in search of food. The wind felt bracing and Bret walked almost to the end of the old stone jetty before turning back toward Spindrift.

Never having been much of a reader, it surprised her that she was looking forward to getting back to her book. She returned to the cottage, settled down and read until she was too sleepy to continue. She put her book down, made a light supper and went to bed.

The next morning it was still overcast, and a brisk wind was blowing. The waves were churning, rushing up onto the beach in curls of foam. Bret decided to take another walk before it started raining again.

At the other end of the beach she saw a man with two children flying kites and stopped to watch for a few minutes. She could hear the delighted voices of the children as their colorful kites rose and danced on the strong air currents. They were having a wonderful time. The man went from one child to the other, a boy and a girl, helping them keep their kites afloat.

What a great dad the fellow must be, the kind of dad every child should have. Strong, playful, fun. The kind Bret wished she'd had. Maybe then everything would have been different. Bret felt the old longing that never seemed to leave her. Subconsciously, in her heart of hearts she'd been looking for someone like that. A guy who wanted to settle down, raise a family, was good with kids.

As she stood there watching the trio, she suddenly realized that the man was Reid Martin. The "good neighbor" from the other night. She felt a pang of disappointment. He was married with children. His wife was probably up at their house preparing a hot lunch for them after they were done flying their kites.

Her disappointment was ridiculous, she told herself. So Reid Martin was married. What should it matter to her?

As all this was going through her mind, Reid turned, saw her and waved.

Bret returned the wave, then abruptly spun around and started back to the cottage.

"Hey, Bret, wait up!" she heard him shout. She halted and waited until he ran the short distance.

He was grinning, his teeth very white against his tan.

"Taking a break from all that heavy reading?"

"You look like you're having a good time," she said. "Cute kids." She nodded to the little girl and boy.

"Yes, they're great." His eyes regarded her steadily. "Jan and Kerry are my brother's children, down visiting me over the weekend. I'm not married."

"Oh." Bret felt a surprising relief—and a stirring of interest. Neat guy, attractive, too. Why had he made such a point of telling her he wasn't married?

She soon found out.

"I was going to stop by Spindrift later today," he said. "My brother and sister-in-law are down here for the weekend and we're having a few people over for a barbecue around six. I just wanted to invite you to come, if you'd like to.''

Bret hesitated. ''Won't I be intruding?''

''Not a bit. These folks are all the year-rounders I was telling you about. We'd really like you to come.''

He seemed eager for her to say yes.

''Okay, thanks.''

''My house is the green-shingled one, the third one down on the beach road.''

''Can I bring anything? A salad? Wine?''

He shook his head. ''Everything's taken care of. Just bring yourself.''

Afterward Bret had to admit she'd had a few misgivings about accepting Reid's invitation. But the evening with the Martin family and some of Reid's close friends was more fun than she could have anticipated. There had been lots of food, barbecued ribs and shrimp kabobs, mounds of coleslaw, iced tea and coffee. No liquor was served. Funny, she never thought she could have such a good time without a few drinks.

Reid's brother and sister-in-law couldn't have been more gracious and friendly, and their children were delightful. Bret had never been around children very much and was surprised at how much she enjoyed them.

Reid walked her back to Spindrift. At the door Bret thanked him. ''It was a lovely evening.''

''It was great having you. How long are you going to be down here?''

''Until the end of the week.''

''Good. Dan and Angie and the kids are leaving tomorrow, so I'll have more free time. Maybe we could have another evening together?''

"Sure. What if I return your hospitality? If you're willing to risk it. Why don't you come for dinner Saturday?"

Reid seemed pleased. "Thanks, I'd like that."

After he left, Bret had second thoughts. Maybe that was a mistake. She had planned this solitary week to get her head on straight, not to socialize. Reid was certainly attractive and interesting, but she hadn't wanted to get involved with anyone. Not for a long time. Then she shrugged. Reid was a nice guy, and one dinner wasn't all that big a deal. What harm would it do to spend another evening with him while she was here?

Bret tried to keep her preparations for the dinner with Reid simple. She bought some pasta, mozzarella cheese and spaghetti sauce, and she could certainly toss a salad. There was ice cream for dessert and of course coffee.

When he arrived early, she was momentarily flustered.

"I was ready, so I just came on over. Couldn't wait," he said in a completely disarming way.

He was so at ease with himself, Bret marveled, since she usually was not until she'd had a few drinks. Reid seemed the sort of man who could feel comfortable anywhere. He looked better than ever in a collarless blue denim shirt and jeans. He followed her out to the kitchen.

"Anything I can do to help?"

"Not a thing, thanks. Everything's done." She'd set the table with Nonie's blue-and-white china. "Just waiting for the pasta to finish cooking." Still feeling somewhat nervous, aware of Reid, she said, "Oh, you could open the wine."

When Reid hesitated, she felt her face redden.

"I'm sorry. You don't drink, do you? Not even on occasion—a special occasion?"

"No, thanks. One drink is one too many for me," he said frankly. "But please go ahead. I always tell people that when they urge me to have a drink. I feel better when they feel free to do what they usually do."

Bret hesitated. She always thought wine made any occasion more festive, more comfortable. But then, Reid always seemed comfortable. She realized it was she who needed to feel less tense.

She wondered if it would be okay for her to have a glass of wine even if Reid didn't. She opened the refrigerator, where the bottle of wine was cooling. "You're sure?"

"Very sure. Bret, I should tell you—and I hope it won't bother you—that I'm an alcoholic. I can't drink."

"Not at all?" Bret met Reid's candid eyes.

"No."

"Well, that's okay with me." She closed the refrigerator. "As a matter of fact, I've been a little worried about my own drinking. Not that I'm an alcoholic. It's just that there have been too many nights and too many mornings when I can't remember where I've been or—" She halted. She wasn't about to spill her heart to a relative stranger. Even as nice a stranger as Reid. No, this was simply a social evening. Nothing heavy. She changed the subject by asking Reid how he happened to live at Sea Watch Cove year-round since it was mostly a summer resort town.

"I'm a technical writer, instruction manuals, that sort of thing. Nothing as romantic as a novelist." He smiled. "I use to live in Richmond, traveling a great deal for my company. Then, when I quit drinking, I launched myself as a freelancer. I write for several different companies, so I can live wherever I want. Have computer, can stay put." He smiled. "I just love this area. When I have to travel, I love coming home, even in the hurricane season or during the winter."

After dinner Bret brought coffee in from the kitchen and saw Reid had picked up the book *Magnificent Obsession* and was thumbing through it.

"Just refreshing my mind on this. It's been a long time since I read it."

"Oh, yes, the book that changed your life, right?" Bret paused, then a little warily asked, "How?"

Reid put the book down and took the cup of coffee Bret handed him. "Well, *Magnificent Obsession* is the story of an alcoholic who did some terrible damage with his reckless driving, causing great harm to several people. How he made restitution and made his life count for something really inspired me to make the necessary changes in my own life." Reid hesitated. "Of course Alcoholics Anonymous was a wonderful support for me and still is."

"You keep going? Even now that you're cured?"

"Alcoholics never consider themselves cured, Bret. We're all in recovery. Which means we're just one drink away from disaster."

Bret thought of all the times she had told herself "I'll just have one," then ended up spending an evening in a hotel cocktail lounge. Not wanting to dwell on that thought, she changed the subject, questioning him about his niece and nephew.

The rest of the evening they talked about various subjects, from world events to their favorite movies. It went pleasantly enough except that Bret felt like there was a twenty-ton elephant in the living room that they were tiptoeing around. The problem of her own drinking.

When Reid got up to leave, she went to the door with him. There, he hesitated as if he had something he wanted to say but then changed his mind.

After Reid was gone, Bret wondered if she had missed a chance. She knew she needed someone to talk to but— *No, I can work it out for myself.*

Ten minutes later there was a knock on the door. Puzzled, Bret opened it and was surprised to see Reid.

"Look, I think I ought to apologize. Like a convert, I tend to proselytize. I may have overstepped my boundaries by talking about my own struggle with drinking and what worked for me. We haven't known each other long enough for me to assume—" He paused. "Forgive me?"

Bret forced herself to look at him, to meet his truth-seeking eyes.

"Of course. No problem."

"Since you mentioned you had some concerns about your own drinking, well, I just want you to know I'm here if you ever want to talk about it."

"Well, thanks, but my main problem isn't drinking just now. It's getting a job. I've got to start seriously job hunting when I get back to Charlotte."

"You sure?"

Bret forced a smile. "I'm sure."

After Reid left, Bret felt sleepy but also wired.

What Reid had told her about a book casually bought
and read bringing about a drastic life change seemed
incredible. But she had no reason to doubt him. She
wondered if she would ever have such an experience.
It didn't seem likely.

It was time for Bret to go, to leave Spindrift. She
had put off long enough facing what had to be faced
back in Charlotte. Looking for a job, finding a
cheaper apartment.

She hated to leave. Resolutely she packed. She decided to take *The Robe,* which she hadn't quite finished, and *Magnificent Obsession,* too. After what
Reid had told her about it, she was curious to read it
herself. She went to get the books out of the bookshelf, and her gaze fell on Nonie's collection of
Bibles. She realized guiltily that she didn't own one.
Nonie had at least a half-dozen, all versions, all trans-
lations—the King James, the New King James, The
New International Revised, The Living Bible. Bret
took that one. She knew it was a simplified version
written in modern-day language.

Just as she was about to take one load of her things
out to her car, there was a knock on the screen porch
door. It was Reid.

"So, all set to go? Can't change your mind, can
I?"

"Don't I wish." Bret sighed. "But duty calls. Or
rather necessity. I have to get back." She affected a
dramatic tone. "Get my life on track. Get a job."

"That shouldn't take long. You're a beautiful, intelligent woman, Bret. Any employer would be lucky
to get you."

"But I don't have much staying power, remember?'' She had told Reid about her series of careers. Told him in a humorous way without giving the underlying reason for quitting or being terminated. ''However, I appreciate the vote of confidence. Can I list you as one of my references on my job applications?''

''Any time.'' He smiled, then added, ''You've got to believe in yourself, Bret. Once I could do that, I was able to turn my life around.'' He went on to explain that although his alcoholism had destroyed his marriage, he'd been able to mend other relationships and get back on a career track.

The conversation was getting a little too personal, so Bret said, ''Well, I'd better be on my way.''

''I get up to Charlotte every month or so,'' Reid told her. ''Will you drop me a postcard, let me know how you are, your address? Maybe we could have dinner or something?''

''Sure,'' Bret promised, though she wasn't at all sure that would happen.

Letter to Anne and Lesley from Bret

I've just gotten back from my week at Spindrift. Here is my report. People who live in Sea Watch Cove are holding on to their cottages even though developers are offering huge amounts for the property. A man I met there, Reid Martin, introduced me to some other year-rounders who feel the developers are planning to tear down all the existing beachfront cottages and build condos. It will ruin the special quality of the place.

Being without a job or income at the moment, I could use the money from a sale, but I

really think we ought to hold on to Spindrift at
whatever sacrifice it might mean until we see
what happens. Okay? We can discuss this when
we meet in September.

In the meantime, wish me luck on my job
hunt!

LESLEY

Badly shaken by Dr. Bates's diagnosis and stern
warning, Lesley didn't want to spend a weekend
alone in her apartment. She had cut short her Christmas vacation because of the debacle of her broken
engagement and had felt guilty for all the distress she
had caused. Maybe going home to Larchmont for a
few days could somehow make up for it.

When she was home, perhaps she'd see Dr. Skelton, their family physician, about her problem. No,
she couldn't go to him.

She could never explain to Dr. Skelton what was
the matter—even if she knew herself. How to explain
this deep emptiness, this hopeless, helpless feeling
that everything in her life was out of control? Except
the one thing she *could* control—what she ate.

It had started the first year she was away at college,
when she had gained fifteen pounds. Her mother had
been a little annoyed that none of the expensive
clothes she had bought Lesley fit her anymore. Adele
had shaken her head. "You really must do something
about your weight, darling."

Humiliated, Lesley had immediately gone on her
first crash diet. She remembered how good she had
felt the first time she had bought a size six. *Trium-
phant* was a better word for it. Everyone had told her
how great she looked, complimented her. It was won-

derful. When she got down to a size four, she had felt even better. Elated when the bathroom scale registered ninety-three.

Too thin? Dangerously thin was what Dr. Bates had said. That scared her. Maybe she should eat more, but when she did she felt sick. Sometimes she threw up.

She wished there were someone she could really talk to, but who? How could she find someone?

When she got to Larchmont early Friday afternoon, her parents were happy to see her. Van was not even mentioned.

The next day at breakfast Adele told Lesley she had a committee meeting for a charity rummage sale that would last for a couple of hours.

Good, Lesley thought, that would give her plenty of time to carry out an idea that had occurred to her early that morning.

Fifteen minutes later Lesley stood on the stone steps of the small redbrick rectory next to Saint Mary's Church. She felt nervous, but she lifted the knocker and tapped it a few times.

She was almost tempted to turn around and run down the flagstone path when she heard footsteps approaching on the other side of the door. The door opened and a tall, slender woman stood there smiling at Lesley.

"Hello."

To her surprise Lesley saw the same woman she had seen that day in the garden months before. Feeling shy, Lesley managed to say, "I'd like to see the priest."

"Come in." The woman opened the door wider.

"I hope I'm not intruding," Lesley said as she

stepped inside. "Maybe I should have called for an appointment? Is the priest available?"

The woman smiled "That's quite all right, and, yes, the priest is available. I'm Sharon Phillips, the vicar of Saint Mary's."

Lesley felt her face flame. "I didn't realize, I'm sorry—"

"Don't apologize. There's no need. I haven't been here that long. I guess I am still somewhat of a novelty. I hope my being a woman doesn't make you feel uncomfortable?"

"No, not at all."

Actually, after her first startled reaction, Lesley felt an immense comfort. The picture of this woman in the garden lingered in her mind. Instinctively she felt she had come to someone who would listen with sympathy, understanding. She felt she had been led here.

"We'll go into the study," the woman said, leading the way down the hall. "Please come in." She motioned Lesley into a pleasant, pine-paneled room with a picture window that looked out on the old-fashioned garden she remembered. "Do sit down." She gestured to one of two plump, cushioned armchairs. "Now, how may I help you?"

"I'm not sure where to begin." Lesley paused. "What shall I call you? Rector? Vicar? I can hardly call you Father…"

"Sharon will do nicely."

Lesley hesitated. She focused her gaze on the olive wood cross with the figure of the risen Christ upon it hanging on the wall directly opposite her.

"It's just that I have this problem about eating," she began to tell Sharon. After that it became easier. She found there was so much she had never faced before, so much bottled up inside—the desire to please, the quest for perfection, the feeling of being manipulated. "The only thing I could control was my weight. It sounds silly and stupid and utterly insane. I guess it is. Sometimes I've really thought I must be crazy."

Sharon made no comment. She leaned forward, her arms on her knees, her chin propped on clasped hands, her warm brown eyes interested, sympathetic, understanding, as Lesley poured out her history.

"To tell you the truth, I'm afraid. The doctor warned me that I was risking my life. But it's so hard for me to eat normally. I've been doing this for years, and it's hard to stop. Sometimes I hate myself, the way I look, but—"

"Lesley, God loves you just the way you are," Sharon said softly. "He created you, the kind of body you have, the bone structure, the perfect size to do what he has put you on this earth to do. So far He has given you good health, which is a gift when you think of the physical burdens some people have. You want to treasure that gift, nurture it, take care of it, not destroy it." She paused. "I gather you are a Christian and have been confirmed?"

Lesley nodded.

"Then I'm sure you were taught that the body is the temple of the Holy Spirit. We must honor it and treat it with respect—yes, with love. Jesus commanded us to love our neighbors *as ourselves!* Remember that. We wouldn't mistreat a friend, or a guest. What is one of the first things we do when someone comes to our home? We offer them refreshment, usually the best food and drink we have avail-

able. We should do no less for the Third Person of
the Trinity who dwells within us.''

All this was said with such quiet assurance that
Lesley could not resent it. It made such sense. Now,
if she could only apply it to her own situation. Not
use her body, her restricted diet, as a kind of rebellion
against the other things in her life she was resisting.

''You are a fine, intelligent young woman, Lesley.
I believe you know what to do and are already aware
of anything I might suggest. My best advice is to pray
about it. Ask for guidance on just how to overcome
this addiction, because that's actually what it is. Just
as gluttony is an addiction to food, this is the opposite—an addiction to starving yourself. Right now it
might seem impossible to break the cycle. But with
God all things are possible.'' Sharon stood up, bringing their discussion to an end. ''I must go and prepare
for our evening service, Evensong. You're welcome
to join us, Lesley. Or you might rather spend a few
minutes alone in our meditation room at the end of
the chapel. And any time you feel the need or just
want to come and talk, please feel free to do so. In
the meantime, you'll be in my prayers.''

''Thank you.'' Lesley rose, too. ''You've helped
me a great deal.''

''I'm glad.'' Sharon accompanied her out of the
room, down the hall and opened the door for her,
saying, ''The side entrance to the chapel is always
open. Goodbye and God bless you, Lesley.''

The door to the meditation chapel squeaked a little
as Lesley pushed it open and entered into the dim
quietness. A peace seemed to gently settle over her
as she took a place in one of the recessed alcoves
along the side. Each had an individual stained-glass

window and a padded kneeler, placed at an angle so all faced the small altar, above which hung a brass cross on which was a molded figure of the risen Christ, arms outstretched in blessing, raised triumphantly.

Lesley slipped to her knees. It seemed appropriate for what she was about to do. To surrender her life. To ask the Lord's help for what she intended to do. The doctor had told her she needed help. She had sought the best help she could find. All her life she had heard that God helps those who help themselves. Lesley felt a strengthening surge of resolve. She would try with all her might, and with God's help, she would make it.

Determined to eat normally, Lesley realized her kitchen was woefully lacking in cooking gear and utensils.

Up to this time, Lesley had done little more than boil water for tea or hard boil some eggs. Now, armed with her new decision to prepare healthy meals, Lesley went, one Saturday morning, to Wadesboro's Kitchen Emporium, a kitchenware store.

At first Lesley stood on the threshold, amazed. This must be a cook's fantasy world. She never knew there were so many things with which to cook or prepare food. Shelf after shelf held cookware and small appliances of all kinds.

Bewildered by the quantity and variety of merchandise displayed, Lesley wandered aimlessly up and down the aisles. After only a few minutes of this she almost collided with a young man.

A glimmer of recognition brightened his eyes, and he said tentatively, "Why, hello."

Slightly taken aback, Lesley murmured, "Hi," wondering why he looked familiar, then turned her attention to the display of cookware on the shelf in front of her. She lifted an aluminum frying pan. But it was too heavy and she replaced it.

"These woks are great for stir-fry," the young man, still standing nearby, volunteered. "I use mine all the time. You can scramble eggs or sauté chopped veggies, throw in some chicken pieces, add instant rice—dinner in a few minutes. Great if you're in a hurry or cooking for one person." As soon as he'd said that, his face got red. "What I mean is—" He halted, then smiled sheepishly. "But then maybe you're cooking for a family?"

Amused, Lesley smiled. "No, just one, just me."

She took a few steps farther along the aisle, but she had lost her concentration. He *did* look familiar, but from where?

She finally chose a blender, an egg poacher, a saucepan and a vegetable shredder. She reached the cash register at the same time as the helpful young man. She hesitated, and he gestured for her to go first. The clerk totaled up Lesley's purchases and put them all in a large plastic bag with the store's name in large red letters.

As Lesley turned to leave, the young man smiled, made a circle with his forefinger and thumb and gave her a cheerful rendition of Julia Child's signoff, "Bon appétit."

Lesley rolled her eyes and laughed.

One thing Lesley knew she needed now in her life was a spiritual foundation to help her remain aware of Sharon's gentle reminder that her body was a temple, that it was her responsibility as a child of God to guard the health she had been given. She had made that commitment; she had chosen life. She intended to keep that promise.

Having decided to find a church, she looked in the newspaper church directory for notices of Sunday services. She remembered passing a small gray stone church called Trinity Chapel, that had reminded her of Saint Mary's in Larchmont. She checked the address and the next Sunday went to the nine-thirty service.

When she entered the sanctuary with its arched beamed ceiling, old oak pews and stained-glass windows depicting familiar Bible stories, Lesley felt this was the right place. There was a comforting stillness as the few attendees came in quietly, then slipped to their knees in private prayer before the organ began playing softly. The minister made his entrance accompanied by two boys attired in red cassocks and starched white surplices.

During communion Lesley recognized the lovely hymn she had heard sung the time she had attended the service at Saint Mary's in Larchmont.

"We will break bread together on our knees,
We will break bread together on our knees,
When I fall on my knees with my face to the rising sun,
May the Lord have mercy on me."

The next verse began, "We will praise God together on our knees..." and this time Lesley joined in.

As she sang along with the other worshippers, she

was filled with a sense of reverence and belonging that was new and infinitely sweet.

After the last blessing the minister made an embracing gesture with his arms and said, "We hope you will all join us next door in the hospitality room for our regular coffee hour. Everyone is welcome."

Leslie hesitated, then decided if she was to become part of this church she needed to put her natural shyness aside and be open to the fellowship it offered.

The women serving coffee from two huge aluminum urns greeted her warmly. When she told them her name and that she was the kindergarten teacher at Wyndham Elementary, one of them seemed delighted. "So you're the Miss Sherwood we heard about all last year! My granddaughter was in your class. I'm happy to see you're human. To hear Melinda tell it, you were some sort of angelic being." They all laughed.

"Very human, I assure you." Lesley smiled.

People behind her were waiting for coffee, so she moved along. She took her cup and looked for a place to sit down when she saw a young man smiling at her from across the room. Was he just showing Christian "agape," welcoming a new member of the church? Then slowly she placed him. Of course, their paths had crossed before. First, in the grocery store with the incident of the French bread, then at the doctor's office, when he'd had his leg in a cast, then at the Kitchen Emporium. What a coincidence. She smiled as he started over to her.

"We're going to have to stop meeting like this," he said in a conspiratorial whisper when he reached her.

"And in such sinister places." She lowered her voice.

"And under such suspicious circumstances."

They both laughed.

"I wasn't sure I recognized you. No cast, no crutches."

"Right. Dr. Bates's office. Then at the Kitchen Emporium, giving unsolicited advice on cookware." His eyes sparkled mischievously. "By the way, how is everything working?"

"Fine. I just dump all sorts of things into the blender, put the top on, push a button, whirr it for a few minutes and it's done. It makes breakfast a whole lot simpler when I'm in a hurry."

"Are you a member here?" He gestured to indicate the church.

"No, I've just started coming," she replied.

"Me, too. Truthfully, I've been church shopping since I moved to Wadesboro. I noticed they have a singles group, but I was a little wary of that—at least, until I attended a service or two, to see if I felt comfortable here."

"And do you?"

"Yes. Do you?"

"The ritual and liturgy are new to me, but I do like it."

"I'm considering taking the hospital ministry course. It's given by this vicar and the hospital chaplain. I want to get involved in something worthwhile." He paused as if he felt he had said too much, been too personal. "By the way, I should introduce myself. I'm Jeff Scott. I work for Benson and McDonough Architects."

"I'm Lesley Sherwood. I teach kindergarten at Wyndham Elementary."

"Now that the introductions are taken care of, could I get you a refill?"

She made a little face. "I don't think so. Coffee in a plastic cup tastes pretty bad."

"Would you care to go somewhere else where the coffee's better? The Pancake House down the street has great coffee, to say nothing of blueberry waffles."

Automatically Lesley's stomach tightened. Then, she thought, *This is a good test. This is what normal people do.* Jeff Scott was an attractive, interesting fellow. He was better looking than she remembered. Handsome, in fact, with a clean-shaven face, blue eyes in which both intelligence and good humor sparkled, a square jaw, nice even teeth. She hadn't noticed before; she'd been too preoccupied with her own problems.

"I'd love to," she replied.

The Pancake House was busy this Sunday morning. They found an empty booth in the back and were soon handed menus by a waitress in a crisp yellow uniform.

Lesley studied the menu, then looked up at Jeff. "What do you suggest?" she asked.

"I'm going with the blueberry waffles," he answered.

Lesley hesitated, mentally figuring how many calories that would be. Then she quickly reminded herself she wasn't doing that anymore. "Sounds good to me, too."

Jeff gave the waitress their order and asked if they could have coffee right away. This was done and his commendation of its quality was soon confirmed.

"Umm, delicious." Lesley savored the rich taste.

"Are you from Wadesboro?" Jeff asked.

"I've lived here since I was hired by the school district—nearly three years. But my hometown is Larchmont."

"Larchmont!" he exclaimed. "My family spent part of every summer of my childhood in Larchmont. My folks rented a cottage on Lake Belmont, and my sister and I attended church camps in Brevard."

Lesley smiled at his evident delight. "Small world, isn't it?"

They went on comparing notes and memories of places and events they had experienced as children in a place familiar to them both.

Their orders came, and Lesley ate more than half of her waffle and drank a second cup of coffee.

"This has been fun," she told Jeff as they left the restaurant and he walked her to her car.

"I hope we can do this again—or maybe something else." Jeff smiled at her. "If you're interested, they're having a retrospective of Humphrey Bogart movies at the Elyseum Theater this week, and Thursday night *Casablanca* is scheduled. Would you like to go with me?"

"Oh, yes. I love old movies."

"Great!" Jeff's smile widened. He pulled a small notebook out of the inside pocket of his tweed jacket. "What's your address?"

She gave him her address on Oak Place. "I have the garage apartment in back of the main house."

"Great. Seven-thirty okay? The show starts at eight."

"Fine, I'll be ready. I'm looking forward to it."

She unlocked her car, and Jeff held the door open

for her. She rolled down the window. "Thanks for breakfast."

"Thanks for coming." He closed the door and leaned on it. Then, in an attempt at a Bogart voice he gave her a small salute. "Here's lookin' at you, kid."

She laughed. "You're very good!" She backed out of the parking space and as she drove away glanced in her rearview mirror. She saw Jeff still standing in the parking lot watching her car.

Chapter Twelve

March and April

A few weeks after what Anne privately called "Dale's defection," she started seeing Elliott Grayson.

One day when she'd come home from work, she'd found a message on her answering machine. "Why is it I have the feeling you're avoiding me?" After a slight pause, it continued, "I have a note from Maddie that she enclosed in my last letter. May I bring it to you? Or better still, maybe I can give it to you at dinner?"

Anne gave his offer some thought and called him back that night. His voice registered the pleasure she was feeling, and they'd made plans for dinner that weekend. They'd been seeing each other since.

The contrast between Elliott and Dale couldn't be more glaring. Elliott was always on time, always kept whatever plans they made, was considerate and thoughtful in a way Dale had never been. Anne realized she looked forward to going out with Elliott. They found a great deal to discuss—books, music, current events. They enjoyed a wide variety of things, such as concerts by the local symphony, and plays. They had even gone together to the college drama department's production of The Belle Of Amherst. And seeing Dale from afar had not caused Anne a single regret.

She could even look back on the experience with Dale with some humor. It had been a good if painful lesson.

At spring break Anne planned to go to North Carolina for her week at Spindrift. She intended to tell Elliott now at dinner.

The Embers had a quiet, intimate atmosphere. Little nooks circled the room around a center stone fireplace in which a fire glowed. For this chilly March night it was perfect. When they were seated at a corner table, Elliott drew an envelope out of his pocket and handed it to Anne.

"Another message from your pen pal." He smiled.

"Maddie? Oh, good, she's quite an artist." Anne already had two of Maddie's creations on her refrigerator. One was a thank-you note she'd sent after Anne's hospitality at Christmas. Last month it had been a Valentine cut out of red construction paper with a frill of paper lace. This one had tissue paper flowers pasted on a pale-green square. Inside was this note: Roses are red, Violets are blue, Sugar is sweet, and Anne is super-neat.

Anne laughed and showed it to Elliott. "How dear of her. I'll cherish this."

"You're on Maddie's A-list."

"She is a darling child, Elliott."

"I'm glad you think so, Anne."

After the waiter took their orders, their conversation focussed on some of the upcoming events at the college for which Anne was writing the promotional material and which Elliott would advertise on the TV station as a public service. It wasn't until they were lingering over their after-dinner coffee that the conversation became more personal.

"Do you remember when we met at Nada and Tom's brunch?" he asked.

"Of course."

"Do you also remember that when I mentioned something about being surprised at the high quality of the promotional material I got from your office, you bristled slightly?"

Anne smiled. "That, too."

"Then you probably also remember you accused me of underestimating the talent at a small college so far from any big city?"

Anne nodded.

"I tried to reassure you by saying I'd already fallen in love with Glenharbor. I believe those were my exact words." He looked at her as if for confirmation. "Well, something more has happened since then." He reached across the table for her hand. "I've fallen in love with you, too, Anne."

Anne drew her breath and tried to withdraw her hand, but Elliott kept holding it.

"Don't, Anne," he said. "Please don't run away."

"Run away?"

"Yes, I think that's what you've been doing. You seem to want to keep our friendship as just that. I feel you enjoy being with me, and yet you seem to be

keeping me at a distance. Am I wrong?'' He paused.
"Ever since Christmas, my feelings for you have
grown. I want us to be together, but I don't want to
go on if it's hopeless. Is it, Anne? I have to know.''

A silence fell as Elliott waited for her response.
Anne was aware of the muted noise of the restaurant
around them, the voices at nearby tables, the clink of
glasses, modulated laughter, the piano playing in the
adjoining cocktail lounge. Gradually everything
seemed to fade, and she heard only the sound of her
own thrumming heart. Suddenly Anne wondered if
this was one of those defining moments in life. She'd
always hoped she'd know it when it happened.

"Elliott, I don't know—"

"Hear me out, please, Anne." His fingers tightened
on her hand. "I think at Christmastime I knew how
much I cared for you, and you cared for us—in a
special way. Maybe you didn't recognize it as love,
just as I didn't at first. Let me explain. I haven't felt
this way before. That's why I know it's right. I know
when it's wrong. My marriage was a mistake—"

"Elliott, you don't have to tell me this."

"I want to tell you. You have a right to know,
Anne. Especially because of what else I want to say.
I know what I feel for you is so entirely different.
Okay?"

She nodded. She could see he was determined to
speak.

"We were young—I was twenty-three, Valerie
twenty-five. I don't mean to sound ungallant, but the
fact is she had been married before and divorced
when we met. Maybe you don't want to hear this, but
I want you to know the truth about me. I'm not proud
of it, but I want to be honest about myself. It's im-

portant for you to know that I've changed.'' He went on. "I wanted to get married, but she didn't. We moved in together and had been living together for about a year when Valerie found out she was pregnant.'' He paused, and Anne could tell this was difficult for him. "I was afraid she was going to get an abortion, and I insisted we get married.

"The truth is, Anne, I was already seeing that we weren't 'made for each other,' as they say. We'd already had a lot of problems. But I did have the basic conviction that life was sacred. I thank God for that. That's one thing I'm not sorry about. I can't imagine not having Maddie. I consider her a wonderful gift.'' He smiled at the mention of his precious child.

"Well, things didn't improve between Valerie and me after Maddie's birth. I had suddenly gotten responsibility and I wanted a steady job, a stable life for Maddie's sake. Valerie was restless—she was used to travel, excitement, new sights, new places, and felt bored with domestic life. She had taken a six-month leave of absence from Worldwide and went back to work within the year. We had a succession of nannies, and I tried to do a lot of my work at home and be with Maddie. But after a while we both saw the end coming. Val was transferred to the East Coast, given the overseas flying assignment she'd always wanted.'' Elliott sighed. "Being separated didn't help. It only intensified our incompatibility. Valerie's schedule allowed her to be off ten days to every five she flew, so it was better for her to keep Maddie. She had good baby-sitters and other help. I had Maddie on my vacations. Not the best arrangement for a little child, but the best we could come up with. When

Maddie started kindergarten, we worked it out for longer visits.''

Their waiter returned to place the check in the small tray beside Elliott's plate and ask if they wanted their coffee refilled.

Elliott took out his credit card placed it on the tray and the waiter disappeared. Elliott took Anne's hand again.

''Maybe this wasn't the right time or the right place, Anne. I hadn't meant to bring all this up tonight. I'd planned to give you the background before I told you I loved you. But I've seen so little of you recently. And being with you tonight is so wonderful and so right, I became more and more convinced that I needed to tell you. I've been afraid you might think I had too much emotional baggage, that I might somehow still be mourning a lost love, a failed relationship. I wanted you to know that isn't the case. I am free to love you, Anne.''

Elliott looked at her with such tenderness, such honesty, such hope, Anne was deeply moved.

''I know what real love is, the kind I could give now. I know what marriage should be, the kind of commitment I'm capable now of making.'' He paused, then said earnestly, ''I do love you, Anne. Maddie loves you, too. Do you think you can find room in your heart for both of us?''

All Anne said slowly was, ''I don't know, Elliott. You know I enjoy your company and I'm moved by your declaration tonight. But I really hadn't thought much about the future. I'll have to reflect on it for a while.''

''That's all I ask, Anne. Please give it some serious thought.''

They left the restaurant and walked out into the parking lot. The moon drifted above the towering trees across a midnight-blue sky. At Elliott's car he got out his keys, then pocketed them again and turned to Anne. He put both arms around her, drew her close. She did not resist. He looked down at her face lit by the moonshine, seeming to search it for a moment, then he kissed her. A very slow, sweet kiss.

In the car he switched on his radio and they drove back to her house in silence, except for the music from the FM station. When they pulled up in front of Anne's crooked little Victorian house, he got out, came around and helped her out of the passenger side. He drew her into the pool of light shed by the street lamp on the sidewalk outside her house. Then he kissed her again.

When it ended she was breathless and a little unsteady. For some reason she realized she hadn't told him about going to Spindrift.

"Elliott, I meant to tell you I'm going away next week. To North Carolina, to my grandmother's cottage on the coast."

"For how long?"

"About a week. During spring break."

"I'll miss you, Anne. While you're gone, will you consider what I asked?"

"Yes."

"When you come back, I want an answer, Anne. I can't keep loving you with no hope."

Anne couldn't go to sleep for a long time. Elliott's question echoed in her mind. Could she really hope that the love he was offering was possible? He seemed to see qualities in her of which she had not been aware. And Maddie loved her, too.

Had Nonie been right when she'd said, "Become the right kind of person, open, generous, kind, and you'll have no problem being loved by the right person"?

Anne had written Bernessa that she was coming for her week at Spindrift. Although the housekeeper had retired after Nonie's death, when Anne let herself into the cottage she found a note from Bernessa that she'd cleared and aired the place and got in a few staples.

Anne carried in her suitcase and stood for a minute in the doorway looking around. Everything seemed to echo with memories of other arrivals. She remembered the excitement, the anticipation of the long summer days ahead. Now, over ten years later, she had that same tingle of expectation. What had Nonie meant for her to get from this week spent alone at Spindrift?

She started unpacking, putting a few things away in the old-fashioned bureau in the room she'd occupied when she was here with her cousins. Then the view from the window caught her attention. The long beach and the curling ocean seemed to beckon. She grabbed a sweater and hurried back down the hall, out through the screened porch, down the steps and onto the wooden walkway over the dunes. At the water's edge, she pulled off her shoes and stockings and let the water curl up and over her bare feet. Then she began to walk along the sand. The salt spray felt wonderful on her face; she felt happy and free. More than she had in ages. She was so glad to be here. Suddenly she asked herself, *What would I do if Spindrift were no longer here?* That was what the three of them would have to decide.

Her first evening alone at Spindrift was going to be a new experience. In the kitchen she surveyed the contents newly stocked by Bernessa, amused to find a box of graham crackers among the staples. It reminded her of bedtime snacks when they were little girls before they went up to the loft. Of the whispered conversations, the sharing of childish dreams before they all drifted off to sleep.

She opened a can of chicken noodle soup and set a place for herself on a table in the front room where she could look out at the ocean and think about what they should do about Spindrift. A beach cottage had to be maintained. To let it stand empty eight months of the year would take its toll on the building. And which of them could spend an entire summer here now?

After she ate she wandered around the front room, checking out the bookcases and shelves. She looked through Nonie's phonograph collection, records sheathed with pictures of stars and celebrities that had once been in the top ten. When Nonie was young, Dinah Shore, Rosemary Clooney, Vic Damone and of course Sinatra had all been at their peak, as well as Peggy Lee. Anne selected one of hers and dusted off the old turntable, switched on the amplifier and listened to Lee's oddly poignant rendering of "Is That All There Is?"

The question begged an answer. She thought of her life over the past ten years. Had she, as Elliott said, run away from life, from love? He was offering her something more than she had ever considered might be possible for her…if she had the courage to take it.

The next morning she awoke to brilliant April sunshine, a perfect Sea Watch Cove day. The tide was coming in, making foamy swirls on the sand, the sky was a cloudless blue. She thought how much Maddie would love it here. She was almost the same age as Anne had been the first year she had come to spend the summer with Nonie.

With the thought of Maddie, the thought of Elliott followed. She knew he, too, would love the peace and serenity of this isolated stretch of beach. Anne wished he were walking along with her now. Did that mean she was in love with him? He had said he wanted an answer when she got back.

Maybe this week she would find the answer. It had to be right for Elliott and Maddie as well as herself. Was she capable of taking on a child, making a home, being a wife?

But throughout the day each time she tried to focus on either of the major decisions facing her, her mind wandered off in all directions.

The third evening at Spindrift Anne curled up on the sagging studio couch to explore Nonie's bulging scrapbooks. There were envelopes containing snapshots, mostly of the three cousins. Every year Nonie had taken pictures of them on the day they arrived and the day they left. Their grandmother had always wanted to see how much they'd grown in the year in between their visits. In shorts, striped T-shirts, barefoot, hair looking for all the world like bleached seaweed, they were standing alongside Nonie. Bernessa must have taken those. Anne stared at the image of her beloved grandmother—the slim, spare figure, biscuit-tan face. Nonie was never idle, moving energetically from one task to the next, the next demand.

Anne marveled, remembering all the activities, all the interests her grandmother had, the organizations to which she belonged or at least supported. There were many of them: guide dogs for the blind, orphans in Chile, endangered rain forests in Nicaragua, missionaries in India.

There were also letters from people Anne had never heard Nonie mention, thank-you notes for some generous or compassionate act of hers. Her grandmother had certainly led a multifaceted life, layers and layers, known only to herself and the people whose lives she touched in so many, unknown ways.

Anne put the scrapbook away. Looking at those old snapshots reminded her of how easygoing their grandmother had been those long-ago summers. Nonie was wonderful about that. As long as they abided by the few house rules, they were mostly on their own. Nonie trusted them and they kept that trust. All that was expected of them was a simple routine each day of making their own beds, picking up their own clothes, fixing their own breakfast, hanging their wet towels and bathing suits on the line outside the back door, and sweeping up any sand they tracked into the house.

The next day and the next Anne spent much the same way. She fell into a rhythm that was both energizing and soothing. Walking the beach, staring out at the sea for long periods of time, thinking deep thoughts. Yet Anne had not reached any conclusions. Not about Spindrift nor about the answer Elliott was waiting for.

In the evenings in the cottage Anne felt most connected to Nonie, remembering that for the last ten years her grandmother had been down here alone.

Everything had a special significance, even the furniture. One evening toward the end of her week Anne went over to Nonie's desk. She remembered seeing her sitting there in the mornings, writing in her journal and day book, penning notes and letters, for she had a large correspondence. Some of the people she wrote to dated back to her boarding school days. Nonie never forgot a friend and seemed to add new ones every summer.

Four of the pigeonholes in the small golden oak desk were empty, the two others held a few postcards and some stamped envelopes. For no special reason Anne opened the small fluted door between them. Inside was a long envelope. Curious, Anne withdrew it and saw that it was addressed "To my favorite granddaughter."

Anne felt her heart beat hard. Should she read it? Had Nonie meant it for *her?* She remembered being hugged and Nonie saying, "You're my special angel, Anne." But wasn't that the title of one of the songs in her record collection? Maybe, she meant this note for Bret, whom Nonie worried about constantly because of her parents' divorce. Or maybe Lesley? Anne held the envelope for a long moment. There was no one to ask. She murmured a silent request for permission, opened it and drew the letter out of the envelope. There was no further clue inside. It just began:

"Dearest one, by the time you read this, I will no longer be a present influence in your life."

How could Nonie ever not be an influence on her? Anne thought. More than anyone, her grandmother had shown her love and empathy, commitment and integrity. She read on.

"You are very special to me. You have many God-given talents I hope you will recognize, and I pray you will use to enrich other lives. Over the years of my life I have learned the purpose of life is not simply to be happy. What is important is to matter in some way. Believe in yourself, respect yourself, your ideals, your goals. These are important, but finding God's will for your life is even more important.''

Tears blurred Anne's eyes. She read on.

''My prayer for you is that you will find love, the love of a good man, with whom you can create a home filled with children, love and laughter. That you will instill in them the values of compassion, honesty and generosity. These are the qualities that make life worth living, a happier, better world for all of us.''

Anne finished reading and sat there for a long time, holding the letter in her hands. She felt a warm sense of peace. Nonie had such wisdom, and she had left these thoughts for one of her granddaughters to find. Or maybe for each of them to find? Anne refolded the letter and put it back in the desk cubbyhole.

Would her grandmother's prayers be answered?

She thought of the words *a good man*. Elliott was certainly that; he had proved it to her in many ways, especially in his devotion to Maddie.

Could they, together, create the kind of home Nonie described? He had asked her to come back with an answer. Was she ready to accept all that committing her life to him involved? Did she love Elliott enough to share the burdens and the joys of parenthood? Did she have the courage?

At the end of the week Anne was packed and ready to go. She looked out at the sea. It had been sunny earlier, but now it was beginning to cloud up, swirling clouds driving away the sun, covering it with a gray milky mist. The best time to leave the beach was a day like this, not so hard as on a beautiful one.

Anne walked through the cottage, said her good-byes to each room. It had been a good week, a re-newing week, and now she thought she had some answers to her questions and Elliott's.

When her plane landed in the San Francisco airport, Anne felt disoriented. Probably because of the three-hour time different between California and the East Coast. Her inner body clock was out of whack.

Her flight for the one-hour trip north to Glenharbor would not leave for another forty-five minutes. She decided to have a cup of coffee while she was waiting. She spotted a coffee shop and as she headed for it, she heard the message over the public address system. It took a while to register that she was being paged. "Miss Anne Sherwood. Please, go to a white courtesy phone. We have a message for you. Miss Anne Sherwood."

She grabbed her things and went back out into the main corridor looking for a white courtesy phone.

"You have a message from Mr. Elliott Grayson. He will meet your flight," the disembodied voice said. Anne replaced the receiver. Her heart was beat-ing fast. Happily.

It was chilly and fog curled around the floodlights and landing field when Anne's plane arrived at Glen-harbor airport. Then beyond the wire fence she saw Elliott waving.

Anne went through the gate and right into Elliott's arms. "I'm so glad you're back." His voice was muf-fled as his mouth was pressed against her hair. But she heard his next words clearly. "I missed you so much, Anne."

He didn't ask for her answer. Could he have forgotten he'd asked for one? "Don't you want to know my answer?"

"I think the answer I was looking for was in your eyes when you saw me. Am I right, or is it wishful thinking?"

"No. I mean, yes, I love you, too," Anne said softly, knowing she had never meant anything more in her life.

BRET

The day Bret got back to Charlotte she did something she had promised herself she wouldn't do. Something she couldn't explain or resist drew her to make a phone call. Holding her breath, she dialed Skip's number, then waited.

"We're sorry. That number has been changed and is unlisted by request of the subscriber," the automated message intoned.

Bret let the receiver slip out of her hand, and it fell to one side, missing the holder. She picked it up and replaced it.

Bret didn't know how long she sat there staring at the phone. She was conscious of the sound of traffic just below, a dog barking. Slowly she covered her face with both hands.

Funny, but she didn't feel like having a drink. Instead, she thought of all the things Reid had told her about his own experiences with drinking.

"They say you have to reach rock bottom before it hits you, what you've done to yourself, to people who care about you, to your life. I had to admit what drinking had done to my life. I'd lost my family, my wife and kids, my job.''

Actually she was in the same boat. She, too, had lost everything that mattered—her job, her lover, her future. She was at rock bottom just as Reid had been.

Bret also remembered the things Reid had said about Alcoholics Anonymous. "Maybe it isn't for you, but at least go to a meeting, try it."

For me? No way? A picture flashed into Bret's mind: Many times when she had driven past the Downtown Rescue Mission, she'd seen the line of down-and-outers, the drunks. And the sign outside— "Get saved, get sober, get soup." Join that bunch of losers? She could stop drinking on her own. At least cut down. She'd proven that while at Spindrift, hadn't she?

First things first, Bret told herself firmly. Get a job, one with regular hours. The kind of job she was good at, the kind requiring creative initiative, personality and imagination was too full of loopholes. She didn't trust herself to go back to her old lifestyle of making her own schedules. What she needed was a routine kind of job that didn't leave her room to get into trouble.

She combed the Help Wanted ads in the paper every day and avoided the jobs that had once attracted her. She marked a couple that were suitable and determinedly applied. One was with Party-Time Caterers, a company that catered banquets, receptions, business buffets. They were hiring waiters and waitresses. "Attractive, personable, responsible men and women ages 18-25. Some experience desirable but not necessary. We will train."

The woman who interviewed Bret was pleasant,

brisk and evidently shorthanded. They needed servers for that very night. A major corporation was holding a large party at one of the big hotels. The duties for that night would be mostly helping the guests find plates and silverware, handing them napkins and telling them what the contents of the various dishes were. The bar would be serviced by professionals.

"Do you have a white blouse, black skirt, comfortable shoes?" was the final question.

Bret hurried back to her apartment to search her closet for the requisite clothes. Dressed and ready to report to the hotel at five o'clock, she surveyed herself in the mirror, thinking, "Well, it's come to this, has it?" All her dreams of glamorous jobs, all the big-time career goals, had dwindled down to being a waitress? She remembered Nonie's often-made remark, "Whatever you do, be the best you can be." She smiled. Okay. Tonight she'd be the best food server she could be. At least it was a job—an honest one and one she was fairly sure she could hold.

The hotel banquet room was like a movie set—the walls were a soft blue, with tall windows draped in shimmering satin, and several crystal chandeliers glittered. Circular tables covered with damask cloths had elaborate flower centerpieces, gilt chairs seated six at each. At one end was the bar. At the other, a crescent-shaped table behind which Bret was stationed, splendidly displayed an array of food fit for a feast in ancient Rome.

The evening turned out to be an interesting learning experience. As a jewelry rep Bret had often attended similar affairs, the memory of which was dim thanks to the amount of wine she had always drunk from the open bar. She couldn't remember much of the banal conversation nor whether much business had been transacted, which was supposed to be the purpose of such occasions.

It was a novel experience to be an observer of the same young executive types and sales reps plying their trades, doing the same sort of thing she used to do.

At the end of this evening, she was tired and her feet ached from standing so long, but she had been paid and had enjoyed talking with the other young people hired with her. Most of them were students, pursuing their education at the local college, working to pay off bank loans or living expenses while they attended classes. Bret decided all were much more worthwhile than some of the forgettable persons she had met as an attendee at similar business or social functions.

After that first event she was called for other jobs. Bret discovered she could have as much work as she wanted. The catering firm was a popular, thriving enterprise. Its owner, a single woman in her midforties, was ambitious. She took almost every function she could schedule and was building quite a reputation in this business-oriented city. Bret never thought she would be satisfied with a job that a few months ago she would have considered menial. Attitude was everything, Bret was beginning to learn.

Since coming back from Spindrift, Bret had been working on her attitude. What Reid had told her about AA became meaningful: One day at a time. She had also tried to read something out of Nonie's Bible. She liked seeing the passages her grandmother had marked or underlined and reading her notations in the margins.

Bret took every offer to work because she didn't like having long evenings to herself. On the ones when she was home she limited herself to two glasses of wine. It proved she was being responsible.

But sometimes on weekends she slipped into her old habits, watching TV mindlessly, sipping a vodka tonic or a large glass of wine.

She knew she was walking a thin line, that if she let self-pity and loneliness get to her, she could go over the edge. The Mondays after those weekends Bret had the hollow feeling that maybe Reid had been more like her than she cared to admit. Maybe she was in the danger zone of being an alcoholic.

"Nothing happens by chance," Nonie was fond of saying. "Most coincidences are divinely orchestrated." Her grandmother believed that everything—circumstances, chance meetings, sitting beside someone on a bus or on a plane—was preordained for some purpose. Bret wasn't sure she believed that. Until the day she passed the large gray stone church.

She'd passed it dozens of times before, never without a small twinge of guilt and the feeling that she should be attending church somewhere. Actually on this day she was walking home from the corner market when something made her stop. She had purchased more than she planned, and the load was getting heavy. She set the large brown paper bag on the low stone wall in front of the church and rearranged the contents, wedging the bottle of wine beside the folded newspaper. As she did, she noticed the framed glassed-in bulletin board in the front of the church. It gave the times of Sunday services. But it was the notice underneath that caught her attention: AA Meeting—Wednesday, 7:00 p.m. Basement.

Bret picked up her grocery bag and walked on. But she could still see that sign as if it were printed in front of her eyes. She put her groceries away, placed the bottle of wine in the refrigerator. Then, surprising herself, she went out of the apartment and back out onto the street and walked the few blocks back to the church.

She went in the massive carved double doors to the dimly lit interior. In the vestibule of the church Bret scanned the leaflet rack. There were helpful pamphlets of all kinds with encouraging titles. Her gaze caught one—"The Twelve Steps." It rang a bell. Of course, Reid had mentioned it. She pulled one out of the holder. The steps were listed with Roman numerals, rather like the way she always thought of the Ten Commandments.

She read the first step: "Admit that you are powerless over alcohol, that your life has become unmanageable." Two: "Believe that only a Power greater than yourself can restore you to sanity." Three: "Decide to turn your life over to the care of God as you understand Him." Four: "Make a searching and fearless inventory of yourself."

Whoa! That was a tough one, something she had been studiously avoiding.

She continued reading. "Admit to God, to yourself and to another human being the exact nature of your wrongs. Be ready to allow God to remove all these defects of character." But could He? Even *hers?* That would be stretching it.

"Humbly ask Him to remove your shortcomings. List all the persons we have harmed and be willing to make amends.'' Bret shuddered. She couldn't even remember the names of most of them. *Of course, my mother, but then she has some amends to make to me and my father....*

Oh, gosh, this was impossible. Bret started to put the pamphlet back in the rack. Then something stopped her. Instead she folded it and stuck it in her pants pocket.

Suddenly Bret's energy was drained. The very thought of going through those Twelve Steps and trying to put them into practice were exhausting. Did people really do it? Wasn't there an easier way to quit drinking? All it took was willpower, right?

Anyway, that kind of program wasn't for her. Sure she drank too much at times, but she wasn't really an alcoholic. The last few weeks she had kept her drinking to two glasses of wine most evenings. That showed she wasn't an alcoholic, didn't it?

Bret almost forgot about the incident during the next two weeks. She had worked steadily nearly every evening at a series of wedding receptions and anniversary banquets. The catering company considered her dependable because she rarely turned down a chance to work.

Her first free Saturday she bundled her basket of clothes down to the apartment laundry room. There were two other women there, both at the folding table. Bret thought they must be friends as they were chatting together and gave Bret only a passing glance when she came in.

Bret quickly sorted through her batch, separating the colored things from white. Before she put a pair of denim pants into the machine, she went through the pockets. She felt something and pulled out a folded pamphlet. It was the Twelve Steps pamphlet she had taken out of the church rack.

She refolded it, stuffed it into her shirt pocket and started the washer. Then, sitting in one of the orange plastic chairs, she took out the pamphlet and began to read it again.

Soul-searching had never been Bret's long suit, but in spite of an inner reluctance she kept reading. The more she read, the more troubled she became.

Some of the questions designed to determine whether you were an alcoholic hit perilously close. If she answered them truthfully, Bret had to admit she fit the profile. At least some of the time.

The steps outlined were so drastic. Who could possibly do them all? Reid had, came the answer. And he had quit drinking.

So would it hurt to go to an AA meeting? See what it was like? If someone as intelligent as Reid had found it helpful, why shouldn't she at least give it a try?

A little before seven the following Wednesday Bret walked over to the church. Still not totally sure that she would attend the meeting in the basement, she went into the church and slipped into one of the back pews. To her surprise people began to come in, the lights went on and the organ began to play. Alarmed, Bret looked around and saw that the choir stalls were filling up. Then a man rapped on a podium at the front. ''All right, let's start with 'Great Is Thy Faithfulness.''' Relieved, Bret realized this was choir rehearsal. The voices began rising in the beautiful hymn she recognized from her childhood. Both Nonie and

Bernessa had often gone around the cottage singing it.

It was soothing to listen to the lyrics that extolled God's faithfulness and mercy. If only Bret could believe them. She felt so needy. Could the Lord really provide her with all the things her life seemed to lack? Purpose, self-control, mercy, hope?

Bret sat there just letting the music move through her, opening her heart to its promise and message. She glanced at her watch. It was nearly seven. If she was going to attend the AA meeting, she'd better go. Almost reluctantly she got up and moved down the aisle to the back of the church, the voices of the choir following her, giving her courage.

Bret went down the stone steps to the basement. She could hear the murmur of voices beyond the half-open door. She hesitated, heart pounding. She heard someone laugh. She took a deep breath and took a step closer to the door. What did she have to lose?

At the door marked AA Meeting she reached for the handle and turned it. She walked into a room hazy with smoke from a dozen cigarettes. Well, okay, maybe she was here to learn how to quit alcohol, but she didn't have to quit smoking...at least not yet.

A middle-aged man with thinning gray hair came toward her, extending his hand, smiling.

"Hi, I'm Ted. Welcome. Have a cup of coffee?"

Bret's first impression of AA was the acrid smell of coffee heating too long, cigarettes and her own tension. But most of all she was aware of the warm acceptance that she felt. People smiled and greeted her, but there was no pressure to participate or get into conversation.

When the meeting was over, people filtered out or

gathered in small groups to drink more coffee and chat.

It was not entirely dark as Bret walked back to her apartment in the soft spring evening. Her mind was busy sorting things out. Was she really an alcoholic? Some of the stories she had heard tonight were much worse than anything she had experienced. And yet, something deep inside her made her know she would go back.

For the next two weeks Bret attended the AA meetings, once even turning down a job opportunity to go to a Wednesday night meeting. She felt driven, to hear more stories, to learn more. Even though she was still not totally convinced she was an alcoholic, the Twelve Steps themselves seemed a good pattern for life.

Bret finished *The Robe*. Reading it, she found that the Jesus whom Demetrius followed—the Jesus whom Marcus discovered too late was the Messiah— became real to Bret. He seemed so much more than the Higher Power they spoke about at AA meetings. She reread the description of the crucifixion in the book. The agony and suffering finally seemed real to her. Tears fell on the pages as Bret thought regretfully of all the years she had ignored and neglected Him, all the years she had wasted.

Reading this book spurred her to seek out the Bible she had brought from Spindrift. One passage Nonie had underlined seemed very meaningful to Bret. It was Joel 2:25: "I will restore the years the locust had eaten."

If only that could happen. Everything in the past ten years could be wiped out. If she could start over.

There was so much she would do and not do. Was it too late?

One Wednesday evening she was in the ladies' room before the meeting when another woman came in. Bret glanced up from washing her hands at the sink, and saw a stunning-looking woman, with iron-gray hair worn in a becoming upswept style. She was perfectly groomed and wearing a nubby knit Chanel suit. She turned to pull a paper towel from the dispenser and Bret noticed her nails were beautifully manicured, painted pale pink.

"Good evening." She smiled tentatively at Bret.

Good evening? That sounded so formal. What was this elegant lady doing down here in the church basement? Bret didn't have to wait long to find out.

The woman glanced at Bret, gave her a shy smile, "I'm Elyse Fenton. This is my anniversary. Two years sober. I'm a bit nervous about tonight's meeting. I'm supposed to tell my story."

Bret stared at her. Elyse looked as though she might be having lunch on the terrace of a country club or chairing a DAR meeting. An alcoholic? Impossible.

The woman gave a soft little laugh.

"Don't look so shocked. You should have seen me two years ago. It's a real miracle I'm here tonight. I guess that's what I'll talk about."

"How—" Bret began, then broke off.

Elyse continued, "Oh, I was in denial for years. I had all kinds of little tricks to conceal my drinking. I thought I'd gotten away with it, too." She shook her head. "Then one day I walked into my living room where members of my family and some of my closest friends were all sitting, and they let me have it! All the things I'd said and done, the ways I had embarrassed and humiliated them. How concerned they were about my drinking."

"What was your reaction?"

"Shock, at first. I thought my drinking was secret, so ladylike." She smiled. "Next I was angry. I felt betrayed." She took a small bottle of lotion out of her handsome leather handbag and rubbed it on her hands. "Of course, it was the best thing that ever happened to me. I don't know whether I'd have survived without that intervention. Anyhow, tonight I celebrate my sobriety—two years without a drink, without wanting one." Her face was suddenly radiant. She picked up her bag and started toward the door. "See you later."

Bret looked at herself in mirror over the sink, gazing deeply into the eyes confronting her. If it could happen to anyone—to someone like Elyse Fenton—she needn't feel so alone. Bret took a long breath, straightened her shoulders, then left the ladies' room.

Two weeks later, at an AA meeting, one man's story in particular affected Bret strongly. She could relate to many of the facets of his addiction and recovery. During the round of applause that came after he had finished telling his story, Bret suddenly felt herself propelled out of the hard folding metal chair. Before she knew it, she had reached the makeshift podium. Her legs wobbled slightly as she heard herself say, "Hi, my name is Bret, and I'm an alcoholic."

LESLEY

After that first date Lesley began to see Jeff at least once or twice a week. Sunday mornings they always went for brunch following the nine-thirty service at Trinity Chapel. To her amazement Lesley found a new freedom in their friendship. For the first time in years she didn't feel any pressure to be anything but herself.

She and Jeff could talk easily about almost everything. They liked so many of the same things. On weekends they sometimes drove out to the sites of some of the houses Jeff's architectural firm was building, and Jeff would point out some of the parts which he had helped design. Or they would stop at garage sales to browse and pick up odd or unique items, laughing over the other's choices. They both confessed to being frozen yogurt freaks and Lesley was gradually getting rid of her ingrained habit of mentally counting calories. They attended a church-sponsored discussion group on characters in the Old Testament and regularly went to the theater that showed movie classics. Whatever they did together was enjoyable.

One night coming out of a showing of *The Portrait of Jenny,* Lesley told Jeff she had loved the story since she had watched it on TV when she was sixteen.

"I wish I'd known you then," Jeff said. "I wish we'd met in high school."

"No, you don't." Lesley shook her head. "You wouldn't have liked me much."

"Why do you say that?"

"I was so…I guess you'd call it introverted. I didn't like very much about myself then. Not my looks, my personality, not my name…"

"What's wrong with your name?"

"Actually, I think it's one of those names that can be either masculine or feminine. I think in England there are quite a few such names and no one seems to think it strange.'' She smiled ruefully. ''But I think the real reason they named me Lesley is because they wanted a boy. I was a disappointment.''

''You could never be a disappointment. Not to *me,* anyway,'' Jeff said.

Old movies weren't their only subjects for discussion. They talked about all sorts of things, including religion. Jeff took the lay chaplaincy course and shared with Lesley the new insights he had gained during the hours he volunteered in the local hospital.

Lesley admired Jeff for his generosity of spirit, his compassion. He was also intelligent and talented and funny. He made her laugh and relax and be natural, a totally new experience for someone who had always strived to be perfect.

In the short space of time they had known each other, Lesley realized what a deep friendship they had formed. She had never felt so comfortable with anyone.

They talked often of wanting to drive over to Old Salem, the restored colonial village near Wadesboro, so one weekend in May they finally went.

The Moravians who founded the town were in some respects ''plain people'' like the Quakers and Amish. Lesley and Jeff wandered along the charming cobblestone streets, watching the artisans reenacting the crafts of candlemaking and woodworking, browsing in the bookstore and the gift shop, where they each bought a cream-colored coffee mug.

Lesley also selected a set of handwoven place mats for her mother and Jeff bought a book describing the Moravian way of life. After leaving that shop they went to the refreshment parlor. While enjoying some of the famous wafer-thin ginger cookies and ice cream, Jeff read some excerpts from the book.

"Listen to this. A couple who wished to be married had to submit their intention to the elders. This was followed by prayerful consideration, and custom of drawing lots was followed. The negative or positive result decided whether permission would be granted for the marriage. If it was positive, the proposal would be taken to the young woman, and she could refuse or accept."

Jeff looked at Lesley over the top of the book. "That sounds pretty risky to me. How does that strike you?" He paused, then said, eyes twinkling, "You're not Moravian by any chance, right?"

She laughed. "No."

"Good. I'd hate to think my proposal would have to be decided by that method."

It was late afternoon when they drove back to Wadesboro. After Jeff left her off at her apartment Lesley kept thinking what a wonderful day it had been and wondering what he'd meant by "my proposal."

Lesley's parents' thirtieth wedding anniversary was in May. They were planning a large celebration. She told Jeff she'd be going to Larchmont over the long weekend, adding, "You'd be more than welcome to come with me."

Jeff hesitated. "Won't you be too busy helping your mother play hostess? I mean, would we have any time together?"

Suddenly Lesley realized how much she wanted Jeff to come, to meet her parents and have them meet him. "We'll find the time," she assured him. Then, teasingly, she added, "Are you sure you're not afraid of being intimidated? Afraid my parents in their ever so polite way will ask difficult questions?''

Somewhere in her mind was lodged the unhappy memory of Craig's visit when he had been put to a relentless if polite interrogation.

''That doesn't frighten me,'' Jeff said with a certain confidence. ''I'll tell you what. I'll drive up Saturday and we'll play it by ear, okay?''

Lesley was alone when Jeff arrived. Her mother was at the hairdresser and her father was playing golf. He suggested they drive around town so he could see the many changes since he had been here as a boy. They stopped to pick up submarine sandwiches and soft drinks so they could picnic at the park just below Sunset Mountain Inn.

The legendary Sunset Mountain Inn was a massive structure of native gray stone with a red-tile roof nestled into a backdrop of majestic mountains. Built in the early part of the century, it soon became host to people from all over the nation. The porch that ran along the front of the hotel overlooked a golf course and beautiful trails that wound through the surrounding magnificent forest.

They walked along one of these trails behind the impressive structure. It was a beautiful spring day, and the surrounding hills were a fairyland of white-and-pink blossoming dogwood. A narrow stream crossed their path and Jeff held out his hand to help Lesley manage the stepping stones to the other side. Still holding her, he stopped and said,

''I meant to wait to say this, Les, but somehow this seems to be the right time, the right place.''

''What is it?''

''Before we met I'd almost given up finding anyone like you. All those times we kept running into each other, I tried to tell myself were just incredible coincidences. But I've come to think they were more than that.''

Lesley started to say something but Jeff held up his hand to halt her.

"Let me finish. All the crazy things that brought us together—my breaking my leg the first day out on my ski trip and ending up in the doctor's office the same day as you. Even stranger is that my appointment was scheduled for another day and I'd changed it, so if Dr. Bates hadn't been delayed at the hospital that day, we would have missed each other entirely. Doesn't that strike you as more than a coincidence?'' Jeff demanded. "Like it says in the Bible, 'Everything works together for good for those who love the Lord and are called to His purpose.' What I'm trying to say is…I love you. And somehow now, in this place that has so many connections for both of us, seems the right time to tell you.''

Lesley felt an inner sense of "At last!" She had found the right person and it was Jeff. Was it too soon after her broken engagement to be so sure? She didn't want to make another mistake.

But she didn't have time to debate or answer that question. Because Jeff was kissing her, a kiss full of sweetness, longing and promise.

That evening she moved through the gala anniversary party in a perfect haze. Every time her gaze caught Jeff's she felt a surge of happiness.

He left the next morning, but Lesley had to stay for the rest of the anniversary events.

When Lesley got back to Wadesboro, there was a

message on her answering machine from Jeff. "Call me the minute you get back."

He must have been waiting by the phone, because he picked it up on the second ring. "I should stay here and work on some plans that will have to be ready when our firm makes a bid on the new recreation center. But I keep getting distracted, thinking of you, missing you."

All her tiredness from the busy social weekend and the long drive faded away. "I missed you, too," she said almost shyly.

Before they hung up they planned to see each other the next evening. Lesley was waiting at her open door when Jeff came bounding up the steps with a bouquet of spring flowers—yellow jonquils and purple irises. Once she saw him, all her uncertainty disappeared. Lesley knew Jeff was the one she had waited for all these years.

For a minute they just looked at each other, everything in their hearts unspoken but somehow understood.

"Come in," she said, stepping back and opening the door wider so Jeff could enter. He put down the bouquet and took Lesley into his arms.

Letter from Anne to both cousins
Surprise! I'm getting married in June and would dearly love for you two to be my bridesmaids just as we used to plan when we were kids. I'll let you know the exact date as soon as it is definite. The wonderful guy is Elliott Grayson, the manager of the local PBS station. He has a darling eight-year-old daughter, Maddie. We are planning a honeymoon in Canada where El-

liott has a media conference in British Columbia. Then Maddie will be spending the summer with us. Do let me know if it would be possible for you to come.

Chapter Thirteen

April–August

Bret could hardly believe how much more alive she felt since she'd quit drinking. To wake up in the morning with a clear head, no worries about what she might have said or done the night before, no regrets. She also looked better—her skin, her eyes, her hair. Life had a new excitement, a new expectancy.

She read the Twelve Steps every day. One of the Twelve Steps was to ask forgiveness, even from someone who had hurt you. Bret thought of her father. Her bitter resentment of him went so deep. Could she ever really get rid of it? He had ruined her life.

Bret couldn't be sure exactly when the birthday gifts and Christmas presents had stopped, although the cards continued for a while signed with just "Your Dad." Until Nonie's funeral Bret hadn't seen her father in years. She hadn't spoken to him since then.

One morning she was reading through Nonie's Bible, the one she had brought from Spindrift, and came across the verse Mark 11:25: "If you have anything against anyone, forgive him so that your Father in heaven may also forgive you. But if you do not forgive, neither will your Father in heaven forgive you."

She had so much to be forgiven for. And *had* been forgiven.

This verse was, after all, like one of the Twelve Steps, another version of the serenity prayer said at every AA meeting.

Forgiveness was her biggest stumbling block. She had always hated Francesca, the woman she blamed for her parents' breakup. Now she realized she had been blaming the wrong person. But forgiving her father was impossible. One summer she'd told Nonie, "I'll never forgive him. Never."

Nonie had just held her for a long time, then said gently, "We have to forgive, honey. Not only because God's Word tells us we do, but because if we don't... There's an old saying, 'He who cannot forgive breaks the bridge over which he himself must pass.'

"He doesn't deserve to be forgiven," Bret had said stubbornly.

Nonie's gentle words came back to her now. She would have to ask her father's forgiveness. She sat staring at the phone, unable to lift the receiver, unable to dial the number written on the card he'd given her at Nonie's funeral. The one she meant to throw away but had kept tucked into her wallet. Sunshine Day

Cruises, Curtis Sherwood, Captain of the *Ho-Hum* deep-sea fishing boat.

She thought of her mother, too. All the Mother's Day cards she had not sent, all the Christmas gifts she had indifferently chosen and mailed. Bret had deeply resented her not coming to the plays, parent-teacher teas, other school events. But maybe it wasn't Gloria's fault. Maybe she couldn't take time off work, afraid of losing her job, not sure the support check would arrive.

Bret recognized that she had been a selfish brat.

She'd blamed her parents for everything that had happened to her since their divorce. Made excuses for herself, her drinking, her own flaws. It wasn't just the drinking. She'd turned that over to the Higher Power, and He had done the hard part, cleaned up her act. Now it was up to her. Could she make up for being a sullen, moody teen? No, but she could ask forgiveness.

She had to make those calls. Do it, whether she felt like it or not. Whether they forgave her or not.

With stiff fingers she tapped out the long-distance telephone number for her father's Florida office.

Bret pulled into her space in the apartment building parking lot. She had just worked a three-hour stint at a conference buffet luncheon at a downtown hotel and felt tired. She couldn't wait to kick off her shoes, slip out of her panty hose and take a long shower. Inside the foyer she checked her mailbox. The surprise announcement of Anne's plans to be married had been followed by a note assuring Bret she still intended to come to the meeting at Spindrift at the end of the summer, to decide its fate. Bret wished she had the money to buy the others out and keep the cottage. She would like to live at Sea Watch Cove year-round as Reid Martin did. Of course she'd have to somehow be self-employed to do that. And where did that leave her? If she just had some talent, some marketable skill she could free-lance. Oh, well! So much for daydreams. She took the mail and went up to her second-floor studio apartment.

A half hour later as she stepped out of the shower she heard the persistent sound of her door buzzer. She slipped into her terry cloth robe, padded to the front room and flipped on the intercom. "Yes, who is it?"

"It's Reid Martin."

"My gosh, Reid! What are you doing in Charlotte?"

"Release the door lock and I'll come up and explain," he replied, and she heard the laughter in his voice.

There was no time to dress. She was standing at her open door when Reid came up the steps. He looked different than he had at the beach. In fact, he looked very handsome wearing gray slacks, a navy hopsacking blazer, button-down shirt and red tie. Used to seeing him only in jeans and cutoffs, Bret exclaimed, "My, my but aren't you all duded up. I hardly recognized you."

He smiled. "You look different, too. Your hair?"

She touched it, laughing. "I got it cut. You know, when in doubt, get a new hairstyle."

"You don't look doubtful. You look wonderful." From behind his back he brought out a bunch of flowers, wrapped in a cocoon of green florist paper.

"Why, thank you, sir." She took the bouquet.

"Come in. You were going to tell me why you're here."

"I thought I might persuade you to go out to dinner with me."

"Oh, Reid, I just got home from work, and I'm dead on my feet. Literally. I've been standing for nearly four hours."

"Doing what?"

"My new job."

"New job? Tell me about it."

"I will if you come in." Reid was still standing in the hall. They both laughed and he stepped in, glancing around the small apartment with interest.

Bret went into the tiny kitchen saying, "I'll put these in water." She turned on the faucet and got a vase out of a lower cabinet. She filled the teakettle, held it up. "Shall I make some tea?"

"Sounds good." He walked around. "Nice place."

"Not very big, but it's all I need. I'm not here all that much. It's kind of empty. It was unfurnished when I moved in. It's uncluttered chic." She laughed. "I've bought a few things. Should have one of those bumper stickers on my car that says Brake at All Thrift Stores. You'd be amazed at what you can find there. The things other people give away! I guess I'm getting the nesting instinct."

She walked back into the living room. "Let me go put something decent on and then we can settle in and talk." She dashed into the bedroom, pulled on jeans and a shirt and came back.

"I haven't answered your question about why I happened to be here in Charlotte," Reid said.

"That's right. Why are you?"

The shrill whistle of the teakettle cut off his reply.

Bret took it off the burner, poured water into the teapot in which she'd placed two tea bags. She put two cups and saucers, sugar and cream on a tray and brought it into the living room where Reid was sitting in one of the overstuffed armchairs. Bret set the tray down on a round oak coffee table. "Okay, now we're settled, so tell me."

He looked at her with raised eyebrows. "Maybe you better tell me just how far this new nesting instinct has gone."

"I just thought I needed to change my ways. Changed jobs, hairdos, living space." She paused. "I thought you were all for change."

"I am. Positive change." He took a sip of the tea she handed him. "Change isn't easy. It's painful, but it can happen and it can be real."

"I think my changes are. Besides all this, I've become a fitness freak. I run, exercise—but maybe that's all surface stuff. I think what you really want to know is have I quit drinking?"

Reid set his cup down, leaned forward. "Bret, I didn't come to check up on you. I just wanted to see you, that's the real reason I came."

"Well, I have quit. I've joined AA. I go to two meetings a week. It's helping me. Not that I'm tempted to slip. And I've quit smoking, too." She laughed. "I'm just too good to be true."

Reid looked at her thoughtfully.

"You sure I can't talk you into going out to dinner? Sounds like you deserve a night out. That's what I had in mind."

"Honestly, no, I couldn't go like this—and I don't feel like getting dressed up to go out. But if you wouldn't mind, we can scrounge up something here. As I remember, you're quite a cook.''

''Is there a deli nearby? I could put together something if you're not too tired to have company?''

''Not at all. I'm glad to see you,'' Bret said, realizing she truly was.

Within twenty minutes Reid was back, two brown paper bags in his arms. A stalk of celery, its leaves like waving green feathers, stuck out the top of one.

''That's a fabulous deli. I got lasagna, salad and dessert.''

''This is incredible. Before you showed up, I was just playing the three wishes game. And number one was that someone would magically provide me with dinner.''

''What were the other two?''

''Someone to listen to me, someone to solve all my problems.''

''Maybe I can also fulfill the second one. I've been known to be a great listener.''

When everything had been put out on the coffee table and they began to eat, Reid asked, ''So, how have things *really* been going?''

It was the opening Bret had been longing for, but now that it was being offered, she wasn't sure she would take it. Maybe she should save it for her AA group. They were all suffering the same kinds of emotions and would sympathize. But could they help? They were all in various stages of recovery, struggling with their own problems.

''It's the Twelve Steps. I'm working the program. I'm on forgiveness.''

''Ah, that's hard.'' Reid nodded. ''It doesn't get easier with practice, either. I should know. I'd hurt a lot of people. As I told you, my drinking cost me my marriage, my family, my kids. They're both grown-up now, but my daughter didn't want me to come to her wedding. Didn't trust that I might not mess up. I'm still working on those relationships.''

Bret told him about her calls to her parents. ''My mother thought I was nuts and my dad was embarrassed, and we just stumbled through our conversation. I don't know whether I felt better after I hung up or not.''

Reid reached out and took her hand. ''All I can say is it takes time. You just have to hang in there.''

They talked about many things; Bret made them more tea. They ate dessert and drank tea and kept talking. Suddenly Reid looked at his watch and stood up.

''It's after midnight. I better be going. It's late and you were tired when I came. I'm going to be here for the rest of the week. I have to make some calls on prospective customers. May I see you again?''

''Yes, of course, I'd like that.'' She smiled and said teasingly, ''Maybe you could go to an AA meeting with me.''

''Maybe I just might.'' At the door he put his hand on her cheek and searched her face. ''I'm awfully pleased to see the progress you've made, Bret.''

Bret felt warmth come into her cheeks. ''Just trying to keep it all together.''

''We all are. Don't forget that. I'll call and we'll make plans.'' He leaned down and kissed her lightly. And then he was gone.

The next evening he took Bret out for dinner. They talked and shared even more. It was both exhausting and exhilarating. Bret had never talked so much about herself nor confided so freely in anyone before. Reid was an incredible listener.

When he brought her to her door, he asked, "Dinner tomorrow night?"

"If it isn't somewhere fancy-schmancy. I'm working a luncheon tomorrow and I'll be pretty tired."

"Your choice. I promise."

"There's a great fifties-style diner not far from here that serves wonderful cheeseburgers and french fries."

But the burgers paled in comparison to Reid's company the next night. They sat in their booth drinking coffee and eventually ordered apple pie and ice cream and talked on and on. As they got up to leave, Reid told her, "I'm going back to Sea Watch Cove tomorrow. Have breakfast with me?"

"Okay," Bret agreed, then said, "You know, when I was drinking, I never used to eat breakfast. Now I wake up ravenous. So be prepared."

As Reid pulled into an empty space beside Bret's small economy car in the apartment parking lot, he shut off the ignition and turned to her. "I haven't told you the real reason I came to Charlotte, Bret. Maybe I wasn't even sure what it was."

"I thought it was to see clients, to get your year's work lined up."

"Not entirely." Reid took her hand. "The real reason was to see you, to find out if what I feel about you was real...and to see if maybe you felt the same way."

Bret's heart began to thrum. At his words all her old self-doubts and uncertainties surfaced.

"Oh, Reid, I could never live up to your expectations of me."

"I don't have any expectations. Almost right away I saw something in you—something special, something I could love. A spirit, a kind of courage that I admired. You've just proved it."

"Don't you mean stubbornness, willfulness?"

"No, much more. And from what we've talked about here recently, you've made some changes that I admire. I've told you about myself, what I was, what I've tried to change, what I still hope to become." He paused. "I think we've both come a long way. Remember the serenity prayer: 'God grant me the serenity to change the things I can and accept the things I cannot change and have the wisdom to know the difference.'"

He lifted her hand and kissed the fingertips.

"I love you, Bret. I think we could make a beautiful life together. What would you say to marrying me?"

Bret wanted to say yes, to trust that, after all, dreams could come true, that prayers were heard. Even for someone like her who had made so many bad mistakes.

"Are you sure?" she asked him in a voice that trembled.

In response, Reid learned forward and she closed her eyes for his kiss. Bret felt a mellow warmth and a comforting assurance. This was a man she could trust, in whose love she would be safe.

Nonie had been right. Happiness was something to do, something to hope for, someone to love. With Reid, Bret knew that every day could be the new beginning that the Twelve Step booklet talked about.

* * *

Before Reid left for Sea Watch Cove she promised him she would think seriously about marriage.

They talked on the phone every night after he went back to the beach. For hours. Bret felt comfortable enough to express her doubts, saying, "Maybe my parents' track record of multiple marriages make 'until death do you part' seem meaningless."

"Don't compare us to anyone else, Bret," Reid said quickly. "For us it will be forever."

Could this be really happening to her? Had she finally been lucky enough to open the right door? Or rather had God opened it for her?

From Lesley to Anne
Sorry to have to miss your wedding, but school doesn't get out until the third week in June, so it is impossible. I hope you will bring your new family to Spindrift at the end of the summer for our reunion and decision-making about the cottage. I agree with Bret about waiting out the real estate boom for a while and keeping Spindrift. We should have no trouble renting it during the summer and we could use the income for maintenance. We can discuss all this in depth when we are together. In the meantime, love and best wishes for much happiness.

From Bret to Anne
I'll be thinking of you on your day of all days. Wish this catering job didn't preclude my being there, but I know you will be a beautiful bride. I hope this Elliott knows how lucky he is.

* * *

Anne and Elliott were married in a rustic chapel with long windows overlooking cliff rocks and sea, with Maddie as Anne's only attendant. Maddie, looking adorable in a blue organza dress with a wide blue satin sash, wore a wreath of tiny blue flowers and carried a basket of trailing ivy and white lilies of the valley. Her shining eyes and angelic smile expressed everything she was feeling.

For the first time in Anne's memory Brenda did not steal the show by her presence. Of course, she looked fantastic, but then so did Anne. Elliott's eyes told her so as she came down the aisle. The pale blue pleated chiffon dress and the miniature orchids in her small bouquet perfectly set off her delicate blond coloring.

For once, Brenda seemed to have nothing to criticize. Not Anne's choice of outfit, not the floral arrangements in the church and especially not the groom.

As Anne listened to the words of the marriage ritual, she felt how rich and deep and true these ancient promises were, as meaningful today as they had been through the centuries. "And keep ye only unto him as long as ye both shall live." When Elliott kissed her, holding her tenderly, Anne knew she was enclosed in a love that would last forever.

They moved into Anne's funky little Victorian mainly because Maddie loved it. "It's like a doll house," she said. She and Anne had had great fun fixing up the room with the slanted ceiling and dormer windows, which would be hers when she came to stay with them.

Anne was happier than she ever thought possible.

This was something she had yearned for all of her life. This was what she had always wanted. What Nonie had wanted for her. She knew it now, recognized it, claimed it.

LESLEY

Lesley spent part of the summer vacation in Larchmont and Jeff drove up several weekends to see her.

Her parents liked him immediately. Lesley was pleased and found it almost ironic.

Jeff was all her mother might have hoped for her. He had impeccable credentials: his family background, his profession, his character and personality. And yet Lesley had picked him herself, or actually God had. As Jeff himself had once remarked, "Everything works together for good for those who love the Lord." He was convinced their meeting had been no accident. Falling in love had just seemed to follow naturally.

Jeff seemed to take it for granted that they would wed. One day he simply said to Lesley, "Where would you like to be married, in Larchmont or at Trinity Chapel?"

Lesley took so long answering, Jeff looked over at her anxiously. "You *are* going to marry me, aren't you?"

"I didn't know you'd asked me."

"I haven't? Well, I'm asking you now. Will you marry me, Lesley?"

She laughed. "That's not very romantic. But of course I will."

"So when and where?" Jeff went on matter-of-factly.

Remembering all the fuss Terry went through over her wedding at Faith and George, Lesley was determined that *her* wedding—hers and Jeff's would be *theirs*—just the way they wanted it. "Well, there's a little church at Sea Watch Cove. I used to go there with Nonie when I was visiting her. I'd like us to be married there."

"Fine. How about if I drive you down there next week?" Jeff suggested. "We'll check it out while we're there, okay?"

Jeff insisted on driving Lesley to Sea Watch Cove for the August week she was going to stay there by herself before Anne and Bret joined her. It was the first time Jeff had seen Spindrift, although Lesley had described it to him often in glowing terms.

He got out of the car, stretched, glanced around. The sea was a deep blue; breakers were rolling into the beach in great curls of foamy white. A few sailboats with multicolored sails skimmed along the horizon.

He came over to her to help her get her belongings and tote bag out of the trunk. He took the wicker picnic hamper out of her hands, leaned down and lightly kissed the tip of her nose. "If your cousins decide to sell Spindrift, let's buy it. It would make a wonderful place for a honeymoon."

"I couldn't agree more."

"And for a family to come to every summer."

She glanced at him shyly. "Your family or mine?"

"*Ours!*" he said and he set the hamper down and this time drew her into his arms and kissed her thoroughly.

When the kiss ended, Lesley sighed. "Oh, Jeff, we're so lucky. I love you."

"And I love you." He kissed her again.

That afternoon they took a long walk along the beach then down the rutted road to the little church of Lesley's memory. It was a white frame carpenter Gothic structure on the hill overlooking a sweep of beach.

They looked at each other. "Do you think it's open?"

They were standing on the steps when they heard a voice say, "Can I help you folks?"

Lesley slipped on her dark glasses to see a tall, lean, bearded man dressed casually in a sportshirt and jeans coming toward them. A fishing creel was slung over one shoulder and he was carrying a fishing rod. As he greeted them, his smile creased his sunburned face into deep lines.

"Hi, I'm Father Luke Simmons. I'm the interim pastor here. The priest's retired. Until the bishop appoints a new pastor to take charge of the parish, we priests in the diocese get a chance to serve here for two weeks at a time." His grin widened. "And have a short vacation as well."

"It's a beautiful little church. I'm Lesley Sherwood, and this is my fiancé, Jeff Scott. I used to come here as a child with my grandmother."

"So, is there something I can do for you?"

"Lesley and I would like to be married here. Would that be possible?" Jeff asked.

"As long as you have the papers signed by your local minister and church."

As they walked back to the cottage along the edge of the ocean, the shallow waves curling around their bare ankles, the sand wet on their toes, they made plans to wed at the tiny church and have the reception at Spindrift. They found a place on the dunes, shel-

tered from the sea wind, warmed by the afternoon
sun, looking out at the sparkling blue sea. Lesley was
sure she had never been this happy.

Much as Lesley tried to hold on to each moment
they were together, the weekend slipped by with
astonishing speed. On Sunday they attended the service at Seaside Chapel, before Jeff had to drive back
to Wadesboro. He put off leaving until the last possible minute.

"I'll be down to bring you back Friday after next,"
he said, tossing his duffel bag in the trunk of his small
car. "You won't forget to put in my offer for Spindrift? Cast my vote, *our* vote?"

"Of course not. I don't think it will be any problem. They'll be happy for me, for *us*. However, I expect Bret will want a cash settlement."

"That can be arranged," Jeff said firmly, then
holding her a few inches back, leaned forward and
kissed her again.

After Jeff left, Lesley stood looking at the empty
road still bearing the tracks of his tires as he'd spun
the wheels a little pulling out of the drifting sand.

She already missed him. She walked down to the
beach thinking of all that had happened between
them, the promises they had made, the future they
were planning together. However, she had not gone
far when she noticed a change in the weather. Clouds
shadowed the beach, gulls were swooping overhead,
their sharp cries filling the salty air with a cacophony
of sound, mingling with the sound of the rough surf.
The farther she went the more overcast the sky became, the wilder the waves grew.

She turned and went back into the cottage, which
now seemed very empty without Jeff. This was the

first time she had ever been alone at Spindrift. The
day outside was rapidly darkening. She shivered and
wondered if she should light a fire in the small pot-
bellied stove. She missed Jeff but knew she had five
days here by herself to fill. There must have been
some reason Nonie wanted each of them to spend a
week here alone. Lesley felt an excited curiosity to
find out what that reason had been.

She walked through the cottage, going from room
to room, meeting memories of herself and her two
cousins' summers here in every one. Back in the front
room she went over to Nonie's desk and idly leafed
through the pages of her desk calendar. There were
notations Nonie had made the last week she was at
Spindrift before her death. "Take flowers to church
for Sunday service" was one.

Lesley remembered going with Nonie to the little
church where she and Jeff now planned to be married.
Bernessa, in a flowered dress and hat, came, too, for
she sang in the choir and often sang a solo. She had
a rich, full contralto voice and when she sang "How
Great Thou Art," Lesley could feel prickles on the
back of her neck. Tucked into the pages of the day
book was also the bulletin from the last Sunday service Nonie must have attended. Then this notation in
Nonie's hand, "O Lord, make Thy way plain before
me. Let Thy glory be my end, Thy Word my rule and
then, Thy will be done."

Lesley ran her hands over the smooth wood of the
desktop. A small fluted door was set within six flank-
ing pigeonholes. Curious, Lesley opened it and drew
out an envelope addressed "To my favorite granddaughter." Lesley's heart began to beat fast. Which
one of them had Nonie meant? Was it for *her?*

As a little girl Lesley had harbored the secret hope that she was Nonie's favorite. Did she have the right to read it? Evidently it had been placed here for one of them to find. Had either Anne or Bret found it during their week here and replaced it for her?

Next weekend her cousins would be here. Should she wait and share it with them? Lesley hesitated but since it wasn't sealed she slipped out the folded sheets of stationery.

"Dearest one," it began, "by the time you read this I will no longer be a present influence in your life. Nor have I been for many years, but that does not mean you have not been held in my heart, occupied my thoughts and been constantly in my prayers."

Lesley's eyes raced down the pages stopping to reread one paragraph twice. "I hope you have found the pearl of great price—an active faith, a satisfying career and, God willing, someone to share life's journey with you."

Through misted eyes Lesley whispered, "Yes, Nonie, I have." She wished her grandmother knew Jeff. She read on.

"Over the years of my life I have learned the purpose of life is not simply to be happy. What is important is to matter in some way. Small things done with a generous heart bring their own special happiness. If I could wish my darling granddaughter one blessing, it would be that she find a way to make a difference, to matter."

There was more and when Lesley finished she read it through again. Then she refolded the pages, put them back into the envelope and returned it to the niche behind the small desk door. If the others had also found it, maybe they could discuss it when they came.

It was late when Lesley went to bed but she didn't go to sleep right away. She lay there hearing the distant pounding of the surf, thoughts coming in waves like the ocean spilling onto the beach. In just this first day, finding the letter, Lesley had begun to understand why her grandmother had asked each of them to stay here for a few days alone.

In the small house, in the quiet hours spent alone, Lesley had the reassuring feeling of the presence of her grandmother's loving spirit. "What you have once loved you never lose." Nonie had given all three of them what they needed for the lives they were to live, however imperfectly—unconditional love, roots and wings.

Lesley was deeply grateful to God for so many of His gifts. First, the gift of a praying grandmother; second, for learning before it was too late to honor the body He had given her; and last but no less important, the love of a good man. By Thursday she was already anticipating Jeff's arrival.

Part IV

Chapter Fourteen

August

It was the last week in August and Anne was packing for the trip east. First there would be the meeting at Spindrift with her cousins. She had already decided that if one or both of the others wanted to keep the cottage, she would give them her share. She and Elliott would hardly make that long trip even once a year to spend time there. Besides, he had several travel plans for them. He wanted to take Anne to some of the places he had already been as well as to explore new places together.

Their honeymoon in British Columbia had been wonderful. Every day she realized more that marrying Elliott was the best decision she had ever made and every day she thanked God for bringing him into her life.

During the time Maddie had spent with them in Glenharbor, Anne had come to dearly love the little girl. She wanted to be the kind of mother to her that she had wanted for herself, to make her feel special and welcome on her visits.

They were taking Maddie with them first to Sea Watch Cove and then to Safari Land in Florida. Maddie was thrilled and told everyone from the sky cap to the reservationist at the ticket counter, "We're on our honeymoon."

Walking between them down the passageway to board their flight, holding on to each of their hands, Maddie gave a little skip. Looking from one to the other, she said, "I just thought of something." She giggled. "I'm not a UAM anymore."

E-mail from Anne to Bret

Elliott, Maddie and I will arrive in Charlotte on Flight 479 Uni-World Airways tomorrow night. Can't wait to see you and have you meet my new family. Looking forward to being with you and Les at Spindrift.

BRET

Bret made a one-night reservation for Anne, Elliott and Maddie at the same hotel where Reid stayed on his business trips to Charlotte. Since her own car was in for major repairs, Reid would be driving them all down to Sea Watch Cove tomorrow for the cousins' reunion.

During the night Bret was awakened several times by the sheer ferocity of the rain beating against her apartment windows. She got up once to crank them closed and saw that the street below looked like a wet black ribbon shimmering in the light from the lampposts. This was more than an ordinary storm, she thought sleepily, glad to crawl back into bed and pull the covers up.

In the morning it was still raining. She went into the kitchen to make coffee and turned on the radio to get the weather report. While rain was welcome to cool things off, as the summer had been unusually hot and humid, this storm was too intense.

The weather report came on. "New storms coming, more rain predicted, more thunder, some lightning, winds up to fifty miles per hour reported along the coast."

Bret looked out the kitchen window. The sky was heavy with hovering clouds like shredded gray cotton; the trees across the parking lot bowed in the strong wind. By the time she finished breakfast, the rain was coming down in torrents, rattling the windowpanes as the fierce wind propelled it. Every so often a clap of thunder split the air. This was the worst storm Bret had ever seen.

When Reid showed up in the late afternoon to go to the airport to meet Anne and Elliott, the rain was still pouring down. They splashed through pools of water on the highway. Flood warnings were erected at several places.

At the airport they found that all flights were either delayed or canceled due to the weather. When they checked, they found that Anne's plane, while delayed, was still scheduled to land in Charlotte. Bret and Reid sat down to wait for Anne and her family to arrive.

"Leaving for the coast tomorrow might not be possible," Reid told Bret. "Seems the winds there are fast reaching hurricane force, and they've already begun evacuation of residents to shelters."

Bret felt a chill around her heart.

"Lesley's at Spindrift, you know. Alone."

LESLEY

Early Friday morning Lesley awoke with a start, not knowing what had awakened her. It was still dark outside. She glanced at the illuminated dial of her travel clock and saw it was only 3:00 a.m. Then she heard the wind, a loud, keening sound that had set the wind chimes on the porch jangling. Rain was coming down in sheets, hitting the windowpanes with force. Lesley pulled the covers higher around her shoulders, drowsily thinking that she and her cousins might not have ideal beach weather for their reunion.

When she woke up later, the wind was still blowing, dashing the rain against the screened-in front porch. It was the worst storm she had ever experienced here. She wondered what time Jeff had left Wadesboro and how soon he would get here. She also worried about her cousins. Anne and her husband and his little girl were supposed to be flying from California and meeting Bret in Charlotte, then coming the rest of the way with her. In her enigmatic note Bret had written that she had a "surprise"—whatever that meant. Anyway, they were all due to arrive sometime this afternoon.

By two that afternoon Lesley was pacing. She had not heard from anyone. The reports she'd heard on the radio before the batteries died were ominous. Hurricane winds were predicted. Telephone lines were down, airports closed. She kept going to the window looking out at the angry ocean, the dark clouds and the relentless rain. It was getting dark. She tried turning on some lamps but nothing worked. The electricity had gone off. Before she could panic, she heard Jeff's familiar car horn.

"Oh, thank God." She rushed out to the porch to hold the screen door open for him, a hard job because the wind almost blew it out of her hands. Jeff jumped out of the car and dashed up the steps and onto the porch. His hair was wet, plastered to his head. Lesley flung herself into his arms. "Oh, Jeff, I'm so glad you're here. I was getting so scared."

"Look, Lesley, you've got to leave here. Right away. There are hurricane warnings for the entire coast. It's all over the radio, plus I passed streams of cars heading inland. Trees are toppled, crews are out repairing lines. It's a matter of hours before Sea Watch will be in the direct path of the hurricane."

"But my cousins…Anne and Bret are on their way here. I can't leave."

"They've got to be aware of the same news wherever they are, Lesley. The highway patrol will be putting up barriers on the roads coming to the coast soon if they haven't done so already. It's serious, honey. We've got to get out of here before we get trapped."

Lesley followed his worried glance toward the beach. Thick, dark clouds hung over an increasingly wild sea.

"Let's check the latest report." From underneath his slicker he pulled out a transistor radio.

"A hurricane building from Puerto Rico and growing into a Category Four is predicted to move with hundred-thirty-one-miles-an-hour winds toward the Caroline coast. Residents in coastal communities are urged to evacuate. The hurricane momentum is at a dangerous rate and is increasing with each passing hour. It is expected to make landfall within the next twelve hours.''

Jeff looked grim. ''I think that's our signal, Lesley. Get your things together and let's get out of here.''

''But what about Anne and Bret?''

''Surely they've been alerted. We'd better get on the road as soon as possible. There'll be lots of traffic heading out, others doing the same thing. Last year's hurricane taught people a lesson about these storms.'' Jeff tried to sound patient but urgency crept into his voice. ''Come on, Lesley.''

She gathered up her belongings as fast as possible, jamming them in a bag helter-skelter while Jeff waited at the front door, tense and obviously avoiding hassling her so as not to make her more nervous.

Lesley stood in the center of the front room uncertainly looking around. Should she take anything of Nonie's, just in case? Her seashell collection, her books, some of her pictures?

''Les, honey.'' Jeff's voice came this time with more urgency. ''Let's move.''

She got the message and grabbed her shoulder bag, slung it over her shoulder, picked up her canvas tote and hurried out the door Jeff was holding open.

The wind was incredibly strong, blowing sand stingingly into their faces as they struggled to get in the car. The roar, combined with that of the wild rush of the waves pounding on the beach below, was almost deafening. Lesley managed to get into the passenger seat and fasten her seat belt. Jeff slammed her door shut, ran to the other side and got in behind the wheel. Rain slashed fiercely against the windshield.

"Pray we make it out to the main road," he said between clenched teeth as he started the engine.

"I am!" Lesley replied, for she had already begun to.

Chapter Fifteen

By the time Bret, Anne and the group got from the airport to the hotel, there was no question but that this was a major hurricane. The coast from Florida to the Carolinas had been declared a disaster area.

They had left a message regarding their whereabouts on Bret's telephone answering machine in case Lesley called.

"I hope she had the good sense to leave Sea Watch before the storm really hit," Bret said to Anne.

"Maybe she went home to Larchmont," suggested Anne.

The hotel lobby was crowded with other refugees from the storm, people dressed in casual vacation clothes who had probably been turned back on their way to the last summer weekend at the beach. Luckily, Bret had booked two rooms. She and Anne and Maddie would take one, while the men would share the other.

"That's okay, I hope?" Bret asked Anne. "After all, you're still practically on your honeymoon."

Anne laughed. "It's fine, really. Anyway, we have a lot of catching up to do. Girl talk." She gave the men a significant glance.

They were all tired and decided to call it a night, not knowing what the next day would bring. A roll-away bed was brought into one of the double rooms for Maddie, who considered it all a great adventure. The adults tried to keep their own concerns under wraps.

Bret had just told Anne of her engagement to Reid when there was a knock on the door.

"It's me! Lesley," the voice called, and Bret rushed to open it.

After hugs and greetings Lesley explained that on their way from the beach, she had used Jeff's cell phone and found out where they were all staying. In a rush, she told them how bad the storm was at Sea Watch.

All three cousins started to talk at once, interrupted each other, laughing, one starting a sentence and another one finishing it. Not to mention congratulating Bret. Maddie watched all this wide-eyed.

Finally she sighed. "I wish I had cousins. It looks so fun!"

The three looked at her, startled, then laughed.

"You will have someday," Anne said.

"And you'll be the oldest," Bret commented.

"Then you can boss the others around," Lesley pointed out.

"Yippee!" Maddie bounced on the cot and gave them all a thumbs-up.

The good cheer continued for a couple of hours, the cousins filling each other in on their lives and introducing their men.

But the mood the next morning was strikingly different. The group sat in the hotel coffee shop, strangely silent. Maddie, the only one eating, looked worriedly from one adult to the other.

Reid, who had been the first one down, had bought a newspaper, and it was being passed around the table for each one to read.

Hurricane hits the Carolinas. Sweeping destruction of beach communities. Winds in excess of 135 m.p.h. High tides reported at 13 to 16 feet. Mandatory evacuation order issued. Impact on waterfront properties enormous. Swath of storm devastating. Thousands of homes destroyed. Power outages widespread. Damage estimated in the billions. Many storm-ravaged towns obliterated in wake of disaster.

It did not bode well for Spindrift.

It was not until late the following afternoon that the coast highways were cleared for traffic, and the Sherwood cousins and the men who loved them and knew how much Spindrift meant to them were able to return to Sea Watch Cove.

They stayed another night at the hotel before setting out to see what damage had been done to their beloved grandmother's cottage.

The sun was out, sparkling on the ocean like tiny gold sequins. The air was fresh and the sky as blue as newly washed denim.

They drove until they reached the wooden barricades. The beach road leading to the main part of the Sea Watch Cove had been washed away. They were told by the highway patrol officer that it was impassable for cars. When they explained they had a cottage on the beach, he gave them permission to check on their property.

The couples walked silently the rest of the way, tense with anxiety about what they would find. But none of them was prepared.

The devastation the hurricane had wrought was visible everywhere. The dunes were flattened, and fractured pieces of lumber, ripped portions of porches and steps and roofs were strewn like so many toy buildings across the sand.

Gripped in emotion, the group moved along the way that had once been so familiar but now looked like a photograph of a war-torn country. Reading newspaper accounts of the destruction was far different from seeing in person the damage left in the hurricane's wake.

When they reached the site where Spindrift had stood, they all stopped. From there the beach stretched emptily in front of them as far as they could see.

Anne felt as if she'd been struck a blow to her chest. She took a ragged breath, shuddering. She felt a tug on her sleeve and looked down to see Maddie's worried little face peering at her through her glasses, her eyes dark and anxious.

"Please don't be sad, Anne," she said in a small voice, slipping her warm little hand into Anne's.

Suddenly Anne remembered Nonie's quote: "Whatever we have once loved we never really lose." That was why memory was such a special thing. All her memories of Spindrift were happy ones. She would never lose them. And there were happy times to come, as Elliott had promised. She had to believe that. She *did* believe it.

Anne reached down and hugged Maddie. "I'm not sad, honey. I'm just sorry you aren't getting to see my grandmother's cottage.

"I love you, Anne," Maddie said.

Over the little girl's head Anne's eyes met Elliott's and she smiled. Out of the mouths of babes, she thought. Love was all that mattered. She had a whole new life to build with these two precious people. Nonie would want her to move on, to find happiness. And she intended to do just that.

Bret felt Reid's hand capture hers, hold it hard. He was sensitive enough not to attempt any platitudes to ease her grief.

The wind off the ocean was chilly. Whitecaps danced on the choppy blue ocean. As she looked out over the empty stretch of beach, Bret felt a hollow feeling in the pit of her stomach. Nothing was left. Spindrift had disappeared into the sea. With it all her hopes, dreams and the promise of a new beginning with her share from the sale of the cottage vanished.

"It's all gone." She sighed heavily.

Reid's arm pulled her close. "Don't feel so bad, darling. We still have my house—it sustained some damage but nothing that can't be fixed. Remember, when we get married, we'll be living just a stone's throw from here ourselves." He paused, then said, "Living by the ocean is always a risk. Just like life itself is."

In her sorrow she'd almost forgotten that Reid's house had escaped the damage suffered by the beach-front cottages. What he said was true. Life itself was a risk, and he was willing to take it with her.

She looked at the beach, washed clean by the tide, stretching out as far as she could see. Here not a piece of driftwood, not a clump of kelp, not a footprint remained. It was as if God was saying yesterday is past, tomorrow awaits, today is the present. A gift. Open it, use it. Forget all that is behind. Leave it all deliberately so no trace of failure, disappointment, bitterness or regret remains.

Bret whispered a prayer of gratitude and thankfulness. "Each day is a new beginning," as the AA booklet said. It was true. She had to believe it, live it.

When Lesley looked at the place where Spindrift once was and realized it was gone, she felt enormous guilt. She should have tried to save something of her grandmother's. In her rush to safety she had left so many precious things behind that were now lost forever.

Jeff put his arm around her shoulder, trying to comfort her.

"Les, honey, the property itself is still here. You three still own it. Another cottage can be built," Jeff said gently. "*I'll* build you another cottage. I'll design it to your specifications. We'll place it a little farther back and a little higher, so it will still have a view of the ocean but will be able to withstand a rushing tide." He began gesturing with his hands, already envisioning the structure in his architect's mind. "In fact, we'll put more windows in it so you'll see the ocean from every room. Maybe even a small cupola on top. Would you like that? Whatever you want, honey."

Through tears at Jeff's sensitivity, Lesley realized

what he was saying. It was a pledge of his love for something she loved.

Spindrift itself—the frame, the wood, the porch— might be gone, but not its spirit. That would live forever in all their memories. And Jeff would design and build another cottage. One that would last another forty years, where they all could come, weeks at a time, and bring their children. Where they could grow old together and watch their grandchildren play and swim and build their own sandcastles.

Epilogue

It rarely snowed in Greenbrae, but early on Christmas Eve a few snowflakes began to drift slowly down. By afternoon the falling snow had made the pines along the driveway up to the Sherwood place look like sugar-coated green gumdrops.

In the kitchen Bernessa took the honey-glazed, clove-studded ham out of the oven and transferred it to a large silver platter, a wedding gift to some long-ago Sherwood bride. She surrounded it with pineapple slices, centered each with a spiced peach and garnished it with parsley sprigs. Then she put her head to one side, admiring her handiwork.

Everything was done now. The jellied cranberry salad was in the refrigerator, the candied sweet potatoes and the green-beans-and-almonds casserole only needed heating when everyone got there.

The three couples had taken Maddie for the special children's service at Miss Nora's church. Bernessa smiled. Wouldn't Miss Nora be pleased that her girls had gathered here for the holidays? The house had come alive again with the sound of laugher, music and happy voices. The spicy smell of the cedar Christmas tree permeated the air, mingled with the scent of bayberry candles and the pine bough swag along the mantelpiece in the living room.

The main purpose they'd all come for was to make decisions about the beach property. After Spindrift was destroyed in the terrible hurricane, no one was sure just what to do. Then last night Lesley's smart young man unrolled the blueprints he'd drawn up for rebuilding it. They all gathered around the dining room table while he explained his ideas and the others made suggestions. Building could begin in March, he told them, and the cottage would be ready for occupancy the middle of June.

"Just in time for our wedding." He'd grinned at Lesley. "To which you're all invited."

Congratulations and discussions followed. It was further decided that each family would have a month's vacation there at alternating times each year, and take turns opening the cottage at the beginning of the summer and closing it after Labor Day.

Bernessa nodded her head in satisfaction. Miss Nora would have been so happy to know that the cousins' memories of their summers at Spindrift were such that they wanted the same kind for their own children.

Speaking of children...Bernessa hummed happily to herself as she got out placemats and napkins. That little scamp, Maddie, had let the cat out of the bag sure enough, while she was helping make cheese biscuits that morning.

"Wanta know a secret, Bernessa?"

"Not if you're not supposed to tell."

"It's a happy secret. Besides, everyone will know in—" Maddie stopped to count her small floury fingers "—in about five months." She leaned forward and whispered, "We're having a baby!"

"Mmm-hmm! Is that a fact?" Bernessa beamed. "My, my, that *is* fine."

No wonder Anne had such a glow about her. Anne had seemed softer, somehow, warmer, more like her grandmother than the others. So *that* was the reason.

Miss Nora would be mighty pleased at how all the girls had turned out. Little Lesley, who used to have a kind of hungry look, now had stars shining in her eyes, showing off her new engagement ring.

And Bret. She'd lost that restless, brittle attitude and had achieved a new serenity. Gotten herself a real nice husband a month ago, too. She'd certainly come up with a surprise announcement as well.

"Reid and I are thinking of turning this house into a bed-and-breakfast," she'd told Bernessa that morning. "You know Uncle Randall planned to sell it, but we hated losing Nonie's house. Reid and I have been talking it over, and we've told the others what we'd like to do. They all seem to think it would be a great idea. Somehow opening this house for guests to enjoy seems to continue Nonie's tradition of hospitality. What do you think?"

"I think that would be a real good idea."

"If we can work a deal with Uncle Randall, would you come and help us?"

Bernessa had pretended to be shocked. "Don't you know I'm retired?"

"At least come and be our supervisor," Bret had urged. "You can show us how to do things the way Nonie would want them done."

"Well, now, that's a possibility." Bernessa was already thinking of her daughter-in-law, Zona, who was a fabulous cook, and her niece, who graduated college with a home economics degree.

At last everything was done. All the girls had to do when they came home was set things out. Bernessa took a final look around, then put on her hat and coat. Now she had to get home to her own house where her children, grandchildren and great-grands were waiting. They'd have their annual potluck and then all go to the candlelight service at their own church.

Before she left, Bernessa turned on the Christmas tree lights. Now they would be shining out through the bay window to welcome the folks home from church.

* * * * *

Dear Reader,

This is a story I've long wanted to write. It's said that every family is dysfunctional in some ways. The Sherwood cousins were no exception. When they were brought back together after ten years of separation for a reunion at their grandmother's beach cottage, Spindrift, an opportunity for healing, growth and faith-building was given to Anne, Lesley and Bret. I hope you will enjoy their story.

Blessings,

Jane Peart

Love Inspired®

A FAMILY FOR TORY

BY

MARGARET DALEY

Victoria Alexander would do anything to help the little girl whose special needs outweighed her own—including marry the child's father! But the pain she'd seen in Slade Donovan's eyes told Tory that his daughter wasn't the only one who needed her. Could God's grace heal all their broken hearts and give Tory the family she'd always longed for?

Don't miss

A FAMILY FOR TORY
On sale March 2004

Available at your favorite retail outlet.

1-800-401-7755
19.99
3 CD's
to Brenda
June 06

Love Inspired®

THE SWEETEST GIFT

BY

JILLIAN HART

HEARTWARMING INSPIRATIONAL ROMANCE

Love Inspired

THE SWEETEST GIFT

JILLIAN HART

Pilot Sam Gardner was next-door neighbor and a friend to Kirby McKaslin when she needed one…and the man she fell in love with. But Sam was the one who needed Kirby to convince him that, despite his painful past, he could have a wonderful future—with her as his wife!

Don't miss

THE SWEETEST GIFT
On sale March 2004

Available at your favorite retail outlet.

Visit us at www.steeplehill.com

LITSG